# Sickness
# of the Night

# Sickness of the Night

by
JOHN PAUL LIGOURI

RESOURCE *Publications* • Eugene, Oregon

SICKNESS OF THE NIGHT

Resource Publications
An Imprint of Wipf and Stock Publishers
199 W. 8th Ave., Suite 3
Eugene, OR 97401

www.wipfandstock.com

PAPERBACK ISBN: 978-1-5326-7061-9
HARDCOVER ISBN: 978-1-5326-7062-6
EBOOK ISBN: 978-1-5326-7063-3

Manufactured in the U.S.A.                                              05/13/19

# Contents

---

# CHAPTER 1

# The Status Quo

---

"Ugh," Bridget groaned, "not again." She reached down and grabbed her brush. This was the third time in less than a minute she had knocked her brush on the floor. She went back to brushing the knots out of her hair. She wanted to make sure she looked good and ready for tonight.

"Everything all good in here?" She heard a man's voice from the bedroom. She turned and smiled at her boyfriend, Ryan.

"Hey," she said putting on the charm.

"Damn," he breathed, "you look . . . amazing." She fluttered her eyelids at him for just a moment before she turned from the mirror and thanked him. "How come you never dress like this on our nights in?" he asked striding over to her.

"Well because you never ask me to," she whispered, running her hands up his back as they held each other intimately.

"Might have to start," he muttered as he leaned over and touched his lips to hers. She felt their lips embrace and her eyes closed to savor the experience.

She and Ryan had started dating over two-and-a-half years ago, both as young professionals in their mid-twenties. Bridget had just come out of a difficult relationship and Ryan hadn't seen anybody serious since his girlfriend through all of college dumped him immediately upon graduation, something he hadn't seen coming. In his own words, he had grown infinitely wiser about women since then. They were a perfect match, Bridget thought, even from early on.

They broke off their kiss, realizing how passionate they had gotten during it, but remained in each other's arm; she started scratching his back tenderly as she realized his hands had slid down her back past her waistline.

"A leather skirt?" he asked, a mischievous look on his face. "Normal girls wear these things?"

"Yes!" Bridget said, equally offended and amused by his jab. "And I know you like it because you say something about it every time I wear it."

He nodded his head in begrudging acknowledgment. "Will I get to see you in it when you get back tonight?" he asked.

"Depends. How late will you stay up for me?"

"As late as I have to." They kissed passionately again. This time when they broke off, Ryan winked and walked back out of the bathroom.

Bridget smiled to herself as he did. Her life was just the way she wanted it to be. Ryan was the man of her dreams, they had almost everything in common: they both loved the same TV shows, playing and watching basketball, and mostly even the same movies, although he had an unusual affinity for superhero movies, which she just did not understand. They both loved the summer and the beach, and they both loved Christmas; they had gotten a real tree the last two years in their apartment despite the $150 dumping fee they had to pay when they got rid of it. But they could afford it.

Bridget worked a well-paying marketing job in downtown Milwaukee, where both of them lived. It wasn't the most engaging career for her, she had to admit, but her supervisor was cool, and she was very close with her coworkers. She actually met Ryan through her job, so it had that going for it, too. One of the first people she met was a married woman who said her husband's best friend was single and looking for a good girl, and Bridget and Ryan were introduced. Ryan worked at a well-regarded engineering firm and was making respectable money of his own even considering the fact he was several years older than her. The two of them had dated for about a year before they decided to get a place together, both thinking it best to wait some time before they moved in together. When the time finally came, they signed a two-year lease in an apartment/condo building in downtown. At first, Bridget wasn't the biggest fan of the place, but she had warmed up to it after a while.

Everything was falling into place for her: she was young, in love, had some cash in the bank, and had one of the nicest apartments in the city.

In all reality, it was the fulfillment of her goals growing up. She wanted a good job, maybe not the highest paying, but one that was fun, one that was worth it and didn't make her groan to get up for it. She had always wanted a nice place, and she wanted to escape the drab uniformity of suburbia, so she moved to the city; it was nice to not have to shovel a driveway, mow a lawn, or any of those other dull, strenuous tasks. And, finally, she had wanted love. It wasn't that she wanted Prince Charming to sweep her off her feet and take her to a magical land—that only ever happened in books and movies. Even from an early age she had learned that life was never a fairy-tale. Instead, all she asked for was a man who would love her, and who she could love in return. But she didn't want to get married. Well, maybe she did when she was younger, but as she grew older, she realized what she really wanted was to be an independent millennial, a woman who had found someone worth sharing life with but never surrendering her life to them.

Bridget finished with her hair and looked herself over. She had to admit, she looked really good tonight. It had been some time since she had put this much attention into getting ready, and she felt amazing for it, just as Ryan had said. Her long, dark hair was extra smooth and shiny tonight because of how much attention she was giving it, and she had put in a few eye drops so she could wear her contacts that showed off her brilliant green eyes. She had worn a nice flowy top because she thought it was cute (but mainly because she was just a little self-conscious about her stomach despite Ryan always telling her she looked "fit"). However, she made sure to wear her favorite "night out" piece of clothing, her leather skirt. It was a little short, but otherwise it just fit so well, and she could show off her favorite part of her body, her long slender legs. Of course, her favorite pair of heels would be a nice compliment to those as well, as well as make her taller than her 5'4" frame (she wished she was 5'7").

All of the sudden a loud buzz filled the apartment, and Bridget rushed out of the bathroom to the door and found some shoes.

"Who's that?" Ryan asked from the couch.

"I told some of the girls we could take a few shots if they would pick me up," she admitted. "We'll only be a little bit, you don't have to leave."

"Okay, cool," he said nonchalantly. "You're gonna wear heels only to go grab the door?"

She stood up, her heels securely on her feet. "Yes, I can't walk downstairs dressed like this with slippers," she answered, acknowledging that she usually went to check people in at the front desk in comfier shoes.

She rushed to the elevator, waited impatiently for it, hopped aboard, and went downstairs to check the girls in. After another elevator ride with her friends, they chatted their way back to the room where they had a shot of whiskey before deciding to have another one, just in case the bars weren't as fun as they were all hoping. They decided on heading to Brady Street to start off the night. It was Bridget's friend Abby's twenty-eighth birthday, and single Abby had a thing for hipsters for which Brady Street had a reputation for attracting.

Abby told them she would meet them on Brady Street, so Bridget's group wound up taking a ride-share and got dropped off smack in the middle of all the bars on the street. Bridget's group got there before Abby, so they decided to pass the time by going inside the nearest place until they showed up.

It was a warm Friday night near the end of September, so the bars were packed with all manner of people, especially—much to the chagrin of the girls—college kids, a few of whom had the misfortune of trying to hit on Steph. Steph was one of Bridget's closest friends, who always seemed to get off by teasing and sharking free drinks from single guys at the bars. Tonight was no different, as the two college boys were easily suckered into buying Steph a drink just before the troop peaced out.

As they shared a good laugh about Steph's ruse, Bridget got a call from Abby that they just got to Brady Street. Bridget and everyone went outside to meet them, and after some happy birthday shouting and tipsy hugs, tried to re-enter the bar. However, the bouncer declared the bar was too full for them all to enter. Steph tried her tricks on the bouncer so that he would let them all in, but he was clearly more seasoned than a couple of dumb college kids. Dismayed, the girls all tried the bar across the street, where the same tale unfolded again. Stupid college kids in the first weekend of semester taking up valuable bar space.

"Well what are we going to do now?" Bridget asked.

"We could go to Mike's on Brady a block down," Abby began, "I've been there a few times. It's a little janky, but it has a big dance floor so we should be able to get in." They all agreed, mainly because it was Abby's birthday and they didn't want to be the ones to ruin the night by picking another bar with no admittance.

The group made it past the bouncer with barely an ID check and entered a dimly lit, wide-open space that was probably a restaurant in a previous life. The place was clearly themed upon Milwaukee as an old steel town, what between the old black and white photos on the wall to some pretty cool decorations that culminated in a full-on gaslight in the corner near the bathrooms. The girls were generally impressed. While the music seemed a little soft and unusual for a Brady Street bar, the place made up for it by having a massive dance floor that took up half of the establishment's space.

The girls made their way straight to the bar, ordering some swift drinks and birthday shots for Abby, and then led the charge on the dance floor. Bridget was having quite a time herself when she suddenly noticed Steph and another friend, Kim, talking in the corner. She stopped dancing and walked over to see if anything was wrong.

"No," Steph said, "Kim just thinks this guy has the eyes for her."

"Oh, yi!" Bridget squealed, delighted that Kim might find a cute guy tonight. Kim was another of Bridget's closest friends, and her strikeout rate with cute guys was more than a little depressing.

"Yeah," Steph added, "Kim tried the yawn trick just now, you know where you yawn and if the guy you're watching yawns right after you it's because he's watching you."

"I haven't done that since high school," Bridget almost laughed.

"Hey, it works no matter your age," Steph retorted. "Anyway, Kim says it's that guy sitting at the bar."

"Which one?" Bridget said, suddenly turning about to see the guy.

"The one at the end of the bar, with the bottle," Steph answered.

It didn't take Bridget long to find him; the bar was having one of those times where no one seemed to be ordering. She spied him and was impressed right away at Kim's choice. He was clearly very tall, had dark eyes and dark hair with a sharp close cut. He had smooth features and a clean-shaven face, and was wearing a rather dapper sweater with his jeans. He was quite cute.

"You have to go talk to him," Bridget said suddenly, turning to face the girls.

"I-I. . ." Kim stuttered, but Steph urged her on as well, and she acquiesced, clearly nervous.

Bridget and Steph squealed in excitement to each other as Kim went over and talked to him. They held each other's hand to take some of the anxiety off. It was hard to tell if Kim and the tall, mysterious stranger were hitting things off right away, as the stranger seemed pretty stoic. But Kim was holding her own between some banter and a flattering laugh here or there. 'How did she not have a boyfriend yet?' Bridget wondered. Bridget answered that question almost right away. It was definitely how Kim dressed. Kim always dressed really cute, but she never looked. . . hot, for lack of a better word. Case in point, tonight Bridget's ensemble had gotten her more than a couple passing glances from the boys. And Steph, she always looked ready to flirt, tonight with sky-high heels, a super short skirt, and a very snug crop top. But Kim, she was wearing a very cute red and yellow floral pattern summer dress with flats. Cute, but actually kind of boring compared to her friends. Bridget frowned to herself. Kim deserved a great guy, and Bridget found herself physically crossing her fingers in hope this guy was one.

All of the sudden Kim threw her arm at her side and stomped back towards the girls; Bridget and Steph turned to each other in dismay.

"What happened?" Steph spoke first.

"Yeah," Bridget chimed in, "It looked like it was going so well."

"Yeah, not at all," Kim said sullenly.

"Well, what happened?" Steph asked bluntly.

Kim took a deep breath before she began. "Okay, so, I went up to him, did that thing where I accidentally bumped into him and then kind of joked about how I can never find a bartender when I need one. He said he had it, called the bartender over, then I said I just needed water. He didn't offer to buy anything, so I asked if he was there often, he said he was, I asked how the music usually was, he said it's fine, so then I asked him if he would dance with me. He said no, he's not a dancer, so I asked if he likes good conversation–"

"That's so smooth," Steph remarked in some awe.

Kim gave a little smile and continued, "I asked, he chuckled and said he did, so I asked him if we could meet up sometime and have a good conversation." Bridget had to admit, that was super smooth of Kim. "He said yes, but he's not available a whole lot. I said that's okay and asked for his number. He shook his head and then said, 'hey, that's my job,' and I said no, I wanted his, but then he asked me for mine, so I just said whatever and started telling him my number." She paused and gave a frustrated grunt. "This was the weird part, he just started nodding, he didn't take his phone out or a pen or anything, he just nodded at me. I gave him, like, half my phone number, but he just kept smirking and nodding like an asshole, so I just gave up and walked away."

Bridget and Steph looked at each other quizzically.

Kim vented at the end of her story. "Why would he do that, I mean, what a dick. Why not just say no, I mean, is being honest that hard?"

The other two girls stared at Kim as they tried to make sense of the situation. There was no denying this was one of the weirder bar stories in the last few years—not even fun, just straight-up weird.

The other girls showed up from the dance floor.

"Hey, what's going on?" they asked.

"Not much, Kim was just talking to a guy," Steph answered.

"Oh, that's great! Did you get his number?"

Kim shook her head.

"Well, Abby wants to try a few other places, the music here sucks. We don't know, like, any of these songs," one of them said

"Okay," Bridget answered. "We can go." She snuck a peek back at the bar to see what the tall, mysterious stranger was doing, but he was gone. She paused to look around, but couldn't see him. Oh well. She shrugged her shoulders and left with everyone else.

# CHAPTER 2

# The Date

---

"**B**rr!" Bridget said with a shudder. "It's colder than I thought it would be."
Ryan slung his arm around her and pulled her tight. She nestled into him, despite how it made her shorten her stride a little bit. It was two weeks after Abby's birthday, and despite the fact that it was early October, an early wisp of winter had found its way to Milwaukee. Bridget knew it was going to be cold, but she hated cold weather; she had always tolerated winter because the city was so beautiful for Christmas.

The restaurant they were going to was very close to the lake and very far from parking, and the options were valet for far more money than it was worth or park it farther away and hike. Bridget, however, was starting to wonder if taking valet would've been worth it now, as she had opted against wearing leggings under her skirt, and the small showing of skin between her boots and her skirt was chilling her whole body because of how biting the wind was.

"It's right here," Ryan said at last.

"Oh, I'm so excited!" Bridget said, her teeth beginning to chatter. "It's been so long since the last time we went on a for real date."

"Yeah, it has," Ryan said nodding. "I'm actually kind of embarrassed by how long it's been."

The two rushed in the door and found the hostess, who greeted them and gladly informed them there was immediate seating. Bridget was even more pleased that they had agreed to go to dinner early. They were seated and given their menus.

"I've never been here," Bridget said, admiring the ambiance of the restaurant, as well as how close they were to the lake, with the cloudy sky growing darker and gloomier, heralding the coming evening. Inside the restaurant was lit by great, golden lamps hanging from the walls and ornate chandeliers hanging from the ceiling. The dark carpet, tables, and chairs contrasted nicely with the decorative, off-white walls.

"I came here last week for a work thing," Ryan began, "and right away I was like, 'man, Bridget would love this place.' Plus the food is really good."

Bridget smiled real big at Ryan as they perused the short menus. By the time the waiter came around, they put in their food orders and one for a bottle of wine.

They stared at each other and smiled for a few moments before Bridget finally asked, "How come we haven't gone on a date in so long?"

"Well," Ryan began, sitting back in his chair and looking up at the ceiling while he gathered his answer. "It's. . . it's a lot of reasons, I think. I mean, I know I've been super busy with work, and you've told me as much about you."

"Yeah," Bridget answered quickly. "Plus, like, we're together so much we don't really need to go on dates as much."

"That's true," Ryan consented. "Before we moved in together we went on a lot more dates."

"Yeah," Bridget said almost longingly.

"But, I mean, we get to spend every day together now, so I think some of it is we don't think we need as many dates because we actually don't need as many dates."

"I guess."

"What?"

Bridget looked at him as if to ask why he asked her that.

"What do you guess?" Ryan followed up.

"Oh, I guess," Bridget stammered for words, "I guess I just miss how often we used to dress up and go get dinner, or go that kayak boat place in Veterans Park, or see a play, you remember *A Christmas Carol* last year? That was so much fun!"

"It was really cool," Ryan admitted.

"We have to get tickets for it again when we get home!"

"We'll have to see when it is first."

"I think," Bridget began probing her memory, "it was the weekend right after Thanksgiving."

"Oh," Ryan said dejectedly.

"Oh?"

Ryan gritted his teeth and inhaled through them. "I, uh, I have to travel that weekend for work. We're flying to Houston, so I probably won't be in town for it."

"What days are you gone?"

"I don't know," Ryan shrugged, "but it's probably the whole weekend. We don't have the travel dates set yet, but my boss told me to keep it open."

Bridget made a pouting face at Ryan's reasons.

"I'm sorry, Bridg," he said after a short pause. They sat in silence as Bridget continued to pout before Ryan started again. "But I do have good news about work."

"What is it?" Bridget asked, somewhat uninspired. Most of these days Ryan's good news about work was just little things here or there that he got credit for. He didn't do a great job of explaining everything well enough for Bridget to get the whole picture, so if he went on too long about whatever it was that was going well, the whole experience quickly became a nodding and smiling practice for Bridget.

"I'm getting pretty close to a promotion," he said smugly.

"No way! That's awesome!"

"Well, I think I am at least. All signs point to yes, right now."

"Oh?"

"Yeah," Ryan began. "So the team I'm working with on this deal, our project sub-leader just got a promotion and he's moving to Kansas. The good news is I was asked to take over for him when he leaves in a few weeks."

"That's so cool!"

"Yeah. And, I mean, Joe, the guy who's moving to Kansas, he was only a project sub-leader for, like, maybe six months, I don't even know if it was that long. And, to be honest, he wasn't even that good. He and I would talk a lot and he usually went with my suggestions, so we'll see what happens to him in Kansas."

"Okay, very nice," Bridget said. "Do you get a pay raise or do you have to work extra hours or something?"

"No, that's the 'meh' part. I mean, I get to be in charge of the day-to-day stuff with the project, which I really want to do, but I don't get paid more or anything like that. It's basically a way of telling people who the next person in line is for a promotion."

"That's still awesome."

"It's probably going to be a few more hours each week, but even without a raise it's so much more worth it because I get to tell people what to do instead of the opposite."

"Okay," was all Bridget could reply because the waiter arrived with their wine. After testing it, the two had their glasses poured.

"But," Ryan began again, "the best part of it is that it looks like the promotion will be in Milwaukee. I did some tracing through the company ladder and it looks like the next domino to fall soon would be here in the city, so we wouldn't have to move someplace crazy or anything. Or at least I wouldn't have to move someplace crazy."

Bridget fell darkly silent, simply nodding for her answer. The truth was, she was covering up a small flare of negative energy; namely, the line, 'we wouldn't have to.' *We.* What made him think she would just drop everything to up and move to Nowhere, Kansas for a promotion that he got. Sure, it's possible she would, even likely she would, but that would be her decision, not his, or even theirs. It was her decision.

This was the real reason she had always wanted love without marriage: independence. She had learned early on the significance and self-determination that comes with being a financially independent woman; she had power, the power to say yes or no. She could agree to something like moving in with Ryan because she *wanted* to, not because she *needed* to. In the same way, she could say no to moving to Kansas with him because out of all the states in America, Kansas ranked somewhere in the mid-forties for places she wanted to move to. Far be it for Ryan to presume she would drop everything for him.

To her, it was never worth it to compromise her independence. Without it, she would lose her own identity, her own sense of self and become a part of someone else's identity, Ryan's identity. What gain was there in that? And that's what marriage was to her, losing her own identity.

In that moment, Bridget reaffirmed her decision to not want to get married, even to Ryan, whom she loved dearly. Hypothetically, in six months—or however long it took for him to get a promotion—if they were married and Ryan was asked to take a promotion in Texas, or Kansas, or wherever, one of them would have to make the decision to walk away from something. Either Ryan would have to pass on his promotion, which would be the equivalent of surrendering all his ambition, or she would have to leave her job and try to find a new one in their new city, which would be almost the equivalent of surrendering her life's work and all of her independence. Sure she could start over, but that was the point, it would be starting over entirely from scratch. Marriage just would not be worth it. With anything as big a commitment as marriage, if there was ever a time it wouldn't be worth it, then it was best left untouched.

All the same. . . she suddenly became very keen to the fact—and very curious, too—that she and Ryan had not talked about marriage even once since their early days. In fact, it had probably been well over a year since they had last discussed anything about marriage. Sure, the last time they had spoken it had been merely to uphold their original beliefs on marriage, namely, that it wasn't necessary or even desirable to them. But all the same, to have been in a relationship as long as they had and to not speak of it for such a long stretch of time, that seemed strange, she realized. She perhaps wondered if she should be warming up to the idea. Or maybe it wasn't a good sign that Ryan had no inclination about marriage or kids like. They hadn't even said the word 'marriage' in any context that she could imagine since then, even when talking about other people.

"What's up?" Ryan asked. Bridget snapped to and realized that she had been totally absent from the conversation, if it had still been going on.

"What do you mean?" she asked, trying to stall.

"You've been super quiet for a bit now."

"Oh, uh, I guess, uh. . . I guess I was thinking about how. . ." she trailed off for a moment. "How our relationship feels like it's grown a little. . . I don't know. Do you know what I mean?" She wanted to test the waters here. It had been too long since they had discussed marriage to the point that its absence was stinging more than if they had talked about it too much. It just didn't seem healthy to her. So, she wanted to try and gauge his interest in it, so she decided to bait him into giving her his thoughts on the state of their relationship.

This time it was Ryan's turn to ask, "What do you mean?"

"Well," she began coyly. "I don't know. It just feels like, I mean, we haven't gone on a date in so long–"

"We're on one now," he said with a cheeky smile.

"I know we are now, but before tonight. We just, I don't know, we don't do anything new anymore, we stick to the apartment a lot, we don't see our friends as often, we haven't taken a trip, even a day trip to, like, Chicago, in forever. We just stay in and watch TV or clean the apartment or something like that. I don't know, that just sounds really boring when you look at it like that."

"But has it been boring?" Ryan asked astutely.

"No, of course not," Bridget said, knowing this was a white lie.

"Then what's the problem?"

"Well," Bridget began, stumbling for words. What was the problem? She was hoping Ryan would have an answer. Immediately, her brain jumped to one word: stale. Was their relationship stale? Had they stopped caring and trying? Was that why neither of them wanted to get married? Or, was it as Bridget thought, that they were so perfect for each other that they never needed to discuss it, they just both understood. But still. . .

Dating for years and never discussing marriage, especially at their ages of twenty-seven and thirty? Ryan was thirty, how did he not feel any urge to father children? Bridget thought the ambition of every man was to have a son to raise. It felt somehow wrong to her.

Bridget finally spoke, perhaps a little more plainly than she should have. "It just feels like we're an old married couple all of the sudden. And we're young, I don't think we should be feeling like that."

"No, I agree. Although I wouldn't say we're 'an old married couple.' We may not have the most exciting lives anymore but we still have a lot of fun with each other," Ryan reasoned.

"Yeah," Bridget answered, deciding to play her hand. "But don't you ever feel like we need to take another step? I mean, we live together, we've been dating for a long time, we really love each other. But it feels, I don't know, like it's missing something. Or we're missing something."

Ryan laughed quietly. Bridget looked at him to convey her confusion at his response. "Look, I don't think that at all. I think we're doing great, nothing's going wrong, everything's going right. But if you have something particular in mind, please, share it with me. I want us to be open. If you want to get a dog, or a shared bank account or whatever, we can talk about that. I mean, we love each other, there shouldn't be any taboo topics between us. But you should remember that part of growing up means living in the real world, and sometimes that means giving up some of our dreams. But hey, we got our dream of finding love." He reached across the table and took her hand. Bridget gave a feeble smile as she grasped back. Ryan had missed the point. Or maybe she hadn't been straightforward enough.

"Yeah," Bridget began, as if to press the initiative again, but suddenly the waiter arrived with their food and served them.

"Oh, wow, you're gonna love this food," Ryan said, already getting started as the waiter departed. Bridget sat pondering her next move. "I'm sorry," Ryan said between mouthfuls, "were you gonna say something?"

Bridget merely shook her head, trying to act casual, and laid her napkin out on her skirt.

# CHAPTER 3

# Mike's on Brady

---

"Brady Street," Steph ordered as she, Abby, Kim, Bridget and a couple other girlfriends of theirs climbed into the extra-large ride-share van. It was the next weekend after Bridget's and Ryan's date, and the girlfriends were back together to make more bad decisions.

"Oh, my gosh, this is so fun," Abby said as she and a few other girls giggled in excitement. In spite of how things began for Abby's party, they had finished the night strong. In fact, it had gone so well, they decided to do another one before the weather got too cold to want to go out again. This weekend was much more conducive for it than last week during the cold snap. The temperature had risen so substantially that the girls were more than happy to bare their legs in defiance of the coming winter.

"I'm so happy we could all get together for this tonight," Bridget said. It had been her idea, although as per usual, Steph had been the one to get it all organized. "Thanks, Steph, for getting it all together."

"Yeah, thanks for the invite, Steph," the girls all said in turn as Steph waved it off.

"It was Bridget's idea so thank her," Steph said nonchalantly.

"I can tell," one of the girls said, "she looks so good. Girl, where did you get that dress? You look beautiful!"

Bridget tugged uneasily at the hem of her sweater dress, trying to pull it lower. "This is really old actually. I think I got it in college." A voice from the back of the van uttered 'In college!?' in disbelief. "Yeah," Bridget continued, "I don't wear it that often."

Truth be told, the dress was a fairly uncomfortable. She had got it in college when she was about ten pounds lighter and actually almost an inch shorter. It had fit well then, but she hadn't worn it too much, as she didn't often have need of a dress that covered her neck and arms yet left almost the entire length of her leg uncovered. It was a rather outgoing shade of red, and she had mostly worn it because she had just bought a new necklace that matched perfectly. Plus she loved the heels she had on that also matched perfectly. Such was the price of looking good.

The van pulled up to the same intersection as the last time they had been to Brady Street, and the girls got out, some of them offering the driver thanks, and looked about the street. They had some trouble deciding where to go first, eventually choosing to bar hop about: have a couple drinks, dance a bit, then move on if the music wasn't great.

They went to the American pub first—where they had salvaged last time—but left very quickly after a couple guys attempted to get very "friendly" on the dance floor. They found their way to the hookah bar a little further down the street and were ecstatic about the music, dancing for quite a while. Unfortunately, the same problem reared its head as a few clearly drunk college guys who were a little too sure of their suaveness overplayed their hands. The girls left almost immediately.

"Ugh, college guys are so annoying. And gross," Steph said. She had been the one that the guys were most adamant about, and Bridget could see why. Between Steph's short, form-fitting dress and boots so tall they almost met the hem, she was the most noticeable person in any room; it also didn't hurt her cause that she was the tallest of the group. Bridget's gaze moved to Kim and, again, felt kind of bad for her. Kim looked very pretty, but was much more conservative in her outfit, with a cute long sleeve shirt and a cute skirt that flowed so nicely when she danced. Bridget also noticed that Kim was the shortest of the bunch, and Bridget couldn't help herself by thinking that—if she were a guy—she would undoubtedly notice Steph first. Bridget suddenly realized she was comparing her friends and felt sick with herself.

The other girls voiced their agreement to Steph's statements about the pariah known as college boys.

"Well, what should we do next? I mean, it's only 11, but. . ." Bridget trailed off. The girls were all either listless or indecisive in their responses.

"We should try one more place," Steph said authoritatively.

"Where should we go?" Kim asked.

"What about Mike's?" Abby asked. All the girls looked at each other, not quite expecting that suggestion. "I mean, it wasn't the best, but at least nobody was being weird with us."

"That's true," the girls admitted before agreeing to head back up the street to Mike's.

"Weird with *you*," Bridget heard Kim mutter to no one in particular. Bridget felt her heart drop a bit, but resolved to make sure Kim had a good time.

They arrived and walked into the dark bar space and looked about. The music was more agreeable than last time and Steph led a small contingent of ladies to the dance floor. Bridget, however, really needed a drink of water, so she headed to the bar, while Kim and Abby went to the bathroom.

Bridget got there and asked for a glass of water. As the bartender filled up her glass she noticed that the bartender looked very *avant garde* with his style, sporting the comb-over with the sides of his head shaved, a thick, but well-groomed beard, and a sporty vest with a tie underneath. 'Wait a minute,' she wondered, 'was he the same bartender as last time?'

She thanked him when he finished and took a long drink, disregarding the straw given her. She plopped her glass down and let out a deep sigh of satisfaction, her brain still turning over if this was the same bartender or not. She looked to the bathroom and to see if Abby and Kim were returning, but saw no friendly faces. To pass the time, she briefly examined the bar in their absence, and to her surprise, she saw the guy that Kim had gone after last time. What did he say his name was? It was something funny. . . Anyway, he had been such a jerk to Kim last time, and Bridget had resolved to make sure Kim had a good time.

Suddenly she conceived a bold idea. She was going to scout this guy out for Kim: work him over a bit, get the goods (and maybe his phone number), then find Kim and give her the scoop. She paused for a moment, wondering how Ryan would feel about her doing this, but this wasn't serious. She was doing this for Kim, no one else. She satisfied herself with that reasoning and smiled. This could be fun.

Standing up from the bar, she put on her best runway strut and went over to the space next to the tall, mysterious stranger at the bar. Bridget leaned in and asked for a Long Island iced tea.

The hipster bartender gave her a funny look, but started making her drink all the same. Bridget pulled out her phone and looked at it, before faking a text message. She finished with a frustrated grunt as she turned on and off the sound button on the side, causing her phone to jingle.

Then she turned to the mysterious stranger next to her and asked, "Hey, my friends got separated on our way here, do you know the name of this bar?"

He turned to her, a look of mild surprise on his face. Then he said, "Mike's on Brady. Did you see the sign on the way in?"

"No, I just followed my friends in here," she said, a little extra honey in her voice. "I didn't even notice that some of them got separated."

"Oh, yeah, uh, it's 1330 E. Brady St." he said. "In case your friends need the address."

"Whoa, how do you know that?" Bridget asked, this time in legitimate surprise.

"I come here fairly often," he said with the faintest trace of a smile.

"Really, I don't know if I've ever seen you here," Bridget said coyly.

The guy turned to her with a crafty grin, "You have. I remember."

"Really?" she asked. "Then we clearly weren't introduced. What's your name?"

"Sly," he said straightforward, turning toward her.

That was his name! 'Wait,' she thought, 'whose real name is Sly? This had to be a joke. Although, maybe he was the kind of guy to make up a name while flirting. Did he have a whole flirting persona? Well, two could play this made-up game name.'

"What's yours?" he asked.

Quickly her brain plumbed the depths of her imagination for a smart nickname, one she could build an alter-ego with on the spot. She tried reaching back into her memory, remembering when she and Ryan first moved in together that they had always used nicknames with each other. She tilted her head and bit her fingernail to buy time.

"Sly, huh?" she asked.

"Yeah," he nodded with all seriousness.

"My name is," she scrambled for anything, then just said the first name she could think of. "Foxy." That sounded like a real name. Or at least as real as Sly.

"Foxy?" he asked with a bemused smile.

"Yes," she said, putting on her best offended act as they relinquished their grip.

"Hmm, sounds fitting," he nodded. He had an air of condescension.

"Oh?" she asked, piqued. "About as fitting as 'Sly,'" she echoed.

He merely stared at her as he readjusted his body to face the bar. As he did she tried to remember the last time that Ryan had called her 'Foxy.' That had been his go-to every time they decided to have a little fun together. But it had been so long. In fact, she wondered, when was the last time he had referred to her by so much as 'babe' or 'honey'?

"So," she started again, trying to dismiss the memories rushing back to her associated with that nickname. "You said you come here often. How often?"

"Often," Sly said cryptically as he nodded sideways, taking a drink. "I know you haven't been here very often."

"Oh, really?" she asked. "How do you know I haven't been here when you haven't been here?"

"You're right, I wouldn't," he said condescendingly. "But how you phrased that makes it unlikely."

"Phrased it?" she asked. "What are you, a linguist or something?"

"No," he said, "but I do keep an open eye and open ear to things. It allows me to read into things better."

"Things?"

"Situations, people, etc."

"What about me? What have you read into about me?"

Sly raised his glass to take another drink, paused, then took a long drink before he answered. "Quite a bit."

"Anything you care to share?" she asked.

"Not right now," Sly said simply.

Bridget was stumped. He was acting the same way he had to Kim last time. Could he actually remember her? Or was he bluffing?

Bridget refocused. She was here for Kim, she had to get Sly's number for Kim.

"Not now, huh?" she asked, biting her lower lip teasingly. "What about another time?"

Sly gave a chuckle. "Like when? The next time you come here a month from now?"

"Maybe," she answered cunningly. "Or maybe you could tell me over a drink sometime."

"I have a drink right now and I don't want to tell you, why would I some other time?" he asked in his patronizing way. He sure had a grating personality. But there was something about him, Bridget realized. Maybe it was that personality that seemed to legitimize him, make her believe he did actually remember her and did know something about her.

"Maybe dinner then?" Bridget asked. "If this place doesn't serve food that is." This was weird, but it was for Kim, she reminded herself.

"Dinner?" Sly asked, possibly taken aback.

"Dinner would be great," Bridget said, seizing the initiative.

Sly simply stared as Bridget fluttered her eyelids at him.

He wasn't giving her anything to work with. "Maybe sometime next week," she followed up as he took another drink of his beer, finishing it off and raising his finger to the bartender, who promptly poured another one.

This was all falling apart right here. She hadn't tolerated his crap for five minutes to come away empty-handed. In fact, why was she even still trying to get his number. Out of the corner of her eye she saw Steph and Kim returning from the bathroom. Neither of them saw her, however, because a super-drunk guy was calling after Steph. Bridget noticed the lingering stares on Steph as they walked by, but poor Kim. Bridget steeled her resolve. She had to do this for Kim. Bridget was so happy with Ryan, and Kim deserved that, too.

"Why don't you give me your number so we can plan something?" she asked.

"We can plan something," he said, much faster than Bridget had expected. "But you'll have to be the one to give me your number."

"Oh, really? A cute girl wants your number and you won't give it?" she asked, really layering on the charm.

"Yes," he said, "but I'm willing to take a *foxy* girl's number."

Bridget took a little offense at that remark, but merely answered, "No, you give me yours." She was at the finish line, just keep it together.

"No," Sly said. "You give me yours. The guy always has to call."

"Fine," she said. "But you have to give me your phone to write it down in."

"Why?" he asked plainly.

She wasn't entirely ready for that question. "So I can make sure that you got it," she answered, unconvincingly.

"If you give me your number, I'll take it down," he said resolutely.

Bridget stared at him, her brain unsure if she was more frustrated with him or more intrigued at his whole demeanor. She recalled Kim's experience with him and realized that he was acting the exact same way. So far it was nearly identical. But here was the proving ground.

"Okay," she exhaled trying to sound even more impatient than she already was. She started telling him her number, pausing after the area code to see if he would start writing it down either on paper or in his phone, but he pulled out neither pen nor phone. After a lengthy pause, she continued with the first three after the area code then paused, again waiting for him to note it down in some way, but he continued to just sit and watch her.

"Are you gonna write any of this down or just smile at me?" she asked pointedly.

"Listen," he said, turning fully to face her and sitting up in the bar stool. "Just because I'm not writing it down doesn't mean I'm not remembering it."

"Oh, really?" she asked, crossing her arms in disbelief and disgust at his offhanded antics. She was at her breaking point with him.

"Yes," he said, clearly flustered by her lack of faith. He promptly recited her number back to her before he continued with, "And, for good measure, your friend on the dance floor over there," he pointed with his long arms directly to Kim, who went without noticing his accusatory indication, "Kim, I still remember her name and her number," and then he confidently recited the first eight of her ten digit phone number. "That is, if *she* was being honest with me." He put slight emphasis on 'she' as if to indicate that he did not trust either of them at this point.

Bridget was in mild shock at how sharp his memory suddenly appeared. Maybe he was legit. Granted, he could just be making Kim's number up because Bridget didn't have it memorized. All the same, the fact he remembered Kim's name at all was telling. How did he know that Kim was her friend? Sure they had walked in together, but they hadn't said anything. Could he possibly remember her from three weeks ago? All of the sudden he went from condescending, arrogant jerk to an enigma.

"Go ahead," he said, "grab your phone and check it if you don't believe me."

Bridget, almost instinctively, reached into the small pocket on her dress and took out her phone, looking up Kim's number and actually had to ask Sly to recite it again, which he did flawlessly for a second time.

"How did you know that we're friends?" Bridget asked in mild shell-shock.

"I see things. And remember them. I saw you and that other girl over there, the one with the stripper boots," he indicated toward Steph, "talking to Kim before and after she came up to me last time." Bridget now had to add 'offended' to the growing list of her emotions, of which, 'bewildered' was still foremost.

"And, just like you," Sly continued, "she refused to believe that I could possibly remember something as simple as a few numbers in a specific sequence. But at least you seemed willing to give me a chance." He raised his eyebrows before re-emphasizing. "Seemed."

A decisive silence fell over them as Bridget was still trying to collect herself over this realization that there was far more to Sly than she knew.

"I'm sorry," Bridget said sheepishly, "for doubting you."

Sly froze solid on his stool, then put his drink back down. Another silence drew between the two before Sly started to thaw.

"Thank you," he said. Another short pause ensued. "Most people don't know how to respond when you don't have a cell phone."

"You don't have a cell phone?" Bridget asked rapidly. Sly shook his head. "Why not?"

Sly shrugged his shoulders to convey apathy. "Well, I mean, I just don't feel like I need one. I mean–"

"Hey!" a voice came from behind Bridget. She turned about and saw Steph walking up to her, her heeled boots echoing more loudly than the music. Behind Steph, Bridget saw the other girls all near the door, most of them on their phone.

"Oh, hey, what's up, Steph?" Bridget asked.

"Hey, we're gonna head out. The music isn't great here and it's getting pretty late," Steph said. Bridget checked her phone and confirmed that it was almost midnight. Steph continued, peeking around Bridget, "If you want to stay here with your new friend–" but abruptly stopped talking.

Bridget turned around and realized that Sly was gone. Totally gone! She scanned the entire back area of the bar and did not see him anywhere. There weren't that many people in the bar to start with, where could he have gone?

"Do you want to stay?" Steph asked slowly, her confusion evident. "Cause our ride is almost here."

"Uh, no, it's. . . it's cool, I'll leave with you guys."

She dejectedly concluded that he must've gone to the bathroom or left, although both of those were a long walk for such a short interlude. She followed Steph to the front door, but paused before she left, scanning Mike's for him one last time.

# CHAPTER 4

# The Engagement

---

"Ugh," Bridget sighed in exhaustion. It was 3:47 on Friday afternoon. Why couldn't it just be 4:00 right now? Then again, she'd been asking that question since 10:48. It was a run-the-clock-out situation on this particular early November Friday, and Bridget was almost at the end of it.

Today's experience was the sum total of her whole week thus far: boring, tedious, and generally unpleasant, and all of this on top of the fact that daylight savings time now meant she would be leaving when it was dark out. The previous week had started well, what with her manager getting swiftly promoted to take his boss' old post. Everyone at work was happy for him, and they even had a small party to celebrate. The position her manager was filling had been vacated when the guy decided to take a job at a different company. Bridget did have to admit, the marketing world was one where jumping to different companies was the fastest way to move up, and her company did have a high turnover rate. By this point she was one of the longest tenured employees in the Wisconsin branch, and she had been hopeful that her name was in the discussion for taking the open management spot (motivated, at least partially, by Ryan's talks of promotion and moving, which still echoed dimly in her memory). Not that she wanted to be manager or anything, but she wanted to be in the discussion for it.

However, in a mere weekend, the candidate search was over, and Bridget was almost furious to see who had taken the management position: Tammy, perhaps the most OCD, most anal, most difficult to work with employee in the branch. At first Bridget had feared it was the decision of her old manager to promote Tammy which would have been a rare misstep on his part. As Bridget learned quickly, however, (thanks to boasts by Tammy), the call had come from higher up the corporate food chain, which left Bridget wondering if the people who promoted Tammy had ever talked with her for more than ten minutes. Sure, Tammy had been there for ten years, and she had a decent track record, but she was abrasive, indecisive outside of making someone do something she didn't want to do, and a general yes-woman to her superiors. That last part had to be the reason she got promoted. While Bridget had been there four fewer years, her work ethic and attendance were decidedly better, and she had taken pride in her ability to work smoothly with others. Apparently management didn't share her thoughts on the value of those traits.

Suddenly, Liz, who worked with Bridget and had actually graduated from the same college as Bridget (although neither of them knew it at the time), was standing behind her in her cubicle.

"Hey, Bridg," she greeted as Bridget turned around.

"Hi, Liz," Bridget said, her boredom apparent.

"Hey, did you hear about Marissa?" Liz asked, her tone implying gossip, which Bridget was all too ready to discuss. Bridget straightened up in her chair.

"Yeah," Bridget answered excitedly. "Good for her, I'm excited."

"Yeah, me, too. . . I guess," Liz said with a tone of wondering.

"You don't think they're good for each other?" Bridget asked, reading Liz's expression. Liz shook her head, and Bridget continued, "Yeah, I guess I don't either really. I mean, he's a nice guy, whatever his name is, Jeremy?" Liz nodded. "But does anybody other than the two of them really think it'll work out?"

Liz laughed. "Ha, we'll find out soon, right. I mean, they've only been dating what, like eight months?"

"If that, I thought it was less than that," Bridget answered.

"Yeah," Liz said leaning in close. "And I heard he didn't even drop to a knee, just opened the box and popped the question."

"No! Oh, my gosh!" Bridget said putting her hands to her mouth. "That's soooo bad."

"I know. It doesn't even look like he has fun with her, so I was really surprised when I heard about it," Liz continued.

"I wasn't," Bridget said simply, finally happy to have something fun and gossipy to chat about. "I mean, Marissa's young, Type A, and probably made him ask her to marry him. I bet she gave him an ultimatum."

"You think so?"

"Totally. I think she just wants to never have to get a real job. She's been an intern here for almost a year."

"True," Liz said simply. "But anyway, Marissa wants to have a party for girls only tonight."

"That's pretty last minute."

"Yeah, but she wants to have people over to her apartment for a house party–"

"Ew," Bridget said in disgust, "I haven't been to house party since college."

"Well she still is in college," Liz continued.

"That's right!" Bridget realized. "Wait, how old is Jeremy."

"He's, like, what, maybe thirty."

"Yeah, they definitely won't make it a year together."

"I know, they haven't even lived together. I mean, how can you really know if you'll work out with someone unless you live together?"

Bridget looked horrified at the thought of people not living together before getting married. "I know, right! That's what Ryan and I are doing."

"Yeah. You two are a cute couple though."

"Oh, thank you," Bridget said, flattered.

"But anyway," Liz continued, "she's having a house party at, like, nine I think I heard, but then she wants to go to the bars after to celebrate."

"I can do that."

"Cool. She wants to go to Water Street."

"College girls," Bridget said shaking her head.

"I know! But we might be able to talk her into Old World Third or something."

"Yeah, let's do that," Bridget said decisively.

"Cool," Liz said, "let's get our celebration on tonight. I'll text you after dinner."

Bridget and Liz parted just as the big digital clock on the wall turned to 3:59. Bridget rolled her eyes and resumed thinking about how soul-sucking work had become.

After sixty grueling seconds of staring at the clock, Bridget swept up her things and bolted to the elevators faster than ever before. She and Ryan had loose plans for a simple night in, but maybe they could have quality time before she left for Marissa's.

As Bridget entered the elevator she had a new wave of thoughts roll over her. It had been a long time since she had something to celebrate. She could remember her younger days in college and as a fresh baccalaureate when people would find any excuse to celebrate something. She loved the Halloween parties and Christmas parties and birthdays and engagements and all of those sorts of things. But lately, there hadn't been many celebrations with her or her friends, other than Abby's birthday a couple months ago. That didn't mean there weren't things worth celebrating, it's just people didn't want to share it. Sure, she had a wedding or two and a baby shower every year, but even if it was a friend, it was always a stiff occasion with boring family, so Bridget really couldn't let her hair down and be herself. One of her college roommates had just gotten engaged a month ago, but she didn't hold a party or a girls' night or anything, she just posted some pictures to social media and left it at that. She didn't call Bridget or anyone else specifically about it, at least to Bridget's knowledge.

Which led to another point: all of her friends were starting to get—she hesitated to say it—lame. Like, old person lame, old married couple lame. All her single friends were getting into relationships (except poor Kim and Steph, although Steph's single status seemed more intentional. . .) and then all of her friends in relationships were getting married, and then all her married friends were having kids—not that either of those things were bad. But all the get-togethers, the weekends, the parties, the social stuff, all of that was starting to dry up, and pretty suddenly, too, it felt. No one seemed to have as much time as they used to have.

Suddenly, a horrible thought crossed her mind: was she starting to get old and boring and lame? She shuddered at that thought as she disembarked from the elevator. Could it be so? Could all of the things she was realizing about her friends be happening to her, or have already happened?

As she got to her car in the parking garage, she did her best to shelve that thought as she got into her car and drove back to her apartment.

Bridget felt an eerily similar feeling at Marissa's party as she had felt at the end of the work day: run the clock out. Marissa's house party was just as bad and drunken as Bridget and Liz and the older girls from work remembered them. It was dingy, cramped, and a song had not been played for its full duration in at least a half-hour because someone always would go over and change the song to "their jam" halfway through.

Bridget had gotten there about thirty minutes ago with the intention of trying to get the party to move to the bars. However, Marissa had committed a serious social faux pas by not only inviting her work friends—girls four to six years older than her—but also all of her college girlfriends. This made the situation immediately clique-y and standoffish, as the college girls were having a blast getting white-girl wasted while the work friends were sipping wine coolers, having been ready to leave for some time.

After a few minutes, however, one of the work friends went over to Marissa and told her they were going to call a ride, then asked where they should go first. Marissa quickly said one of the bars on Water Street, but Liz propositioned a place on Old World Third. Marissa said she didn't know where that was so just stick with Water Street and then a lively debate ensued (Old World Third being just across the river). The discussion went on far longer than anyone wanted it to and threatened to go on indeterminately until Bridget finally stepped up and proposed Brady Street rather forcefully. Surprised, the girls rather quickly agreed to that compromise, and Bridget, Liz and the other work girls called for a ride and headed for Brady Street.

They arrived and the girls went to the hole-in-the-wall bar in the middle of the street, but the college girls and Marissa were not too far behind, and a few confused calls and texts later, they were all back in the cold; due to their late arrival on Brady Street, once again, the girls found that their group was going to be too big to all go to one bar.

By this point, Bridget knew the easy solution: Mike's.

The girls wondered aloud about Mike's while Bridget coolly led the way. She knew, as usual, that there would be room for them and plenty of it. The part she left out when she was telling them about it, of course, was that the music the last two times had been so bad it had forced them to leave.

The girls got into the bar and Bridget found it surprisingly busy, and she was equally impressed at the music playing. The girls were more than happy to take to the dance floor while Bridget stood there, somewhat surprised at this transformation. Granted the bar looked the same as ever—even the same bartender was there—but the music was. . . awesome. Bridget followed a couple work friends to the bar where they could finally order real drinks as opposed to the cheap cinnamon whiskey available at Marissa's house. As they ordered, Bridget scanned the bar and was unsurprised to spy another familiar face: Sly, right there in the middle of the bar, just where she had left him two weeks ago. Or, more correctly, where he had mysteriously left her. The memory of their parting came back to her, and she recalled how strange his sudden disappearance had been.

As much as she didn't want to admit it, that had been a factor in her proposing Brady Street. Water Street was for drunk college girls, and Old World Third was fine, but kind of sketchy. Brady Street was a logical alternative, and Mike's then was the obvious destination for a group of their size. But, despite all of the sense it made, Bridget had reluctantly admitted some of the reason she wanted to go to Mike's was to see if Sly would be there. How had he disappeared like a ninja last time? And why was he here—by himself completely alone, no less—for the third time that she was here? It was all so. . . interesting, if very strange.

Bridget looked around and gladly noticed some of her friends had started flirting with a couple cute hipsters at the bar. Bridget was momentarily fixated on another of her friends going after the bartender, who simply smiled at her attempts and said nothing, merely walking away. Bridget then noticed that all of her work friends were either talking with cute guys or nowhere to be found, and she was not about to go searching the bar for them. She ordered a drink and—thinking of nothing better to do—slid over to Sly's section of the bar, taking the open spot next to him.

"Excuse me, is this spot open?" she asked flirtatiously.

Sly turned just far enough to see her out of the corner of his eye, "Hello, Foxy."

At first she didn't even remember giving him that name, but it quickly came back and she went back into character, "Hello, Sly." He remained silent as she waited for a response so she decided to take the initiative with the conversation.

"So, last time, when you just left me standing in the bar alone. Where did you go?" she asked, deciding a frontal assault was the best tactic.

He paused, still without looking at her, before answering simply, "I don't remember what you're talking about."

"Oh, really?" she asked, almost pleased that he said that. "The guy who can remember a phone number for three weeks can't remember what he did to leave a girl standing all by herself?"

He paused again, pensively this time. "I left," was all he said in response before turning to her. "And, as I recall, I didn't leave you alone, I left you with your friend, the dominatrix lady." Bridget gave an offended gasp, as her familiar feeling of frustration with him came back to her. That emotion was stymied, however, as she suddenly realized how frighteningly accurate his description of Steph might be. She was able to snap her brain back into the moment and respond.

"Hold on, you left? Like, left the bar? All the girls were standing by the exit, none of them saw you. . ."

"Yeah. Because they were all on their phones. Ergo, why I don't have one," Sly stated matter-of-factly. Bridget had to pause and realized that he had won this round, despite her best efforts. Refusing the yield the initiative, however, she pressed on against him.

"You seemed to leave in a hurry."

"I have long strides," he replied nonchalantly.

"Were you going to meet someone?" she asked.

"No. I just wanted to leave," he answered.

"I always see you here alone," she pressed. "Do you have a special someone in your life?"

"No," he answered, a flash of frustration in his voice now. Bridget smiled, thinking she was finally getting to him. "And I don't have plans to change that any time soon."

"Really?" she asked, in genuine surprise. "You don't want a special someone in your life at all?"

"No," he reiterated, just as serious as the last time he said it.

"Everyone should want someone special in their life. What kind of person wants to be alone forever? They couldn't be human, right?" she asked, trying to bait him.

She was immensely surprised to see his immediate response was to laugh, a legitimate laugh. Bridget stared at him in involuntary bewilderment.

Then he simply responded, "Maybe." He took a drink before he resumed. "Or maybe I don't want a girlfriend clinging to me because she would always be dragging me along to places I don't want to go and with people I don't want to go with. Just like tonight."

"I wouldn't drag my boyfriend along everywhere with my friends," she snapped back at him.

"Well the only way would be to get a special guy yourself and find out," he shot back.

She crossed her arms and stomped her foot on the ground before lashing back at him. "For your information, I do have a special someone."

Bridget nearly exploded as he seemed to almost spit out his beer. But he beat her to a response.

"Do you flirt with him as much as you flirt with me?" he asked calculatedly.

She was fuming, ready to lose it at him. "Yes! His name's Ryan, and we've been together for almost three years, and we're getting married soon!" The words barely escaped her mouth before she wondered what came over her. What did she just say?

Sly was clearly very taken aback by her outburst and he fell into an almost bashful silence. While he was silent, Bridget's mind was racing. Did she really just say that? Where did that come from? Why would she say that? What was he gonna say to her about that? Her last question was answered first.

His eyes were immediately drawn to her balled up fists. "You don't have a ring though," was his simple reply.

She had no defense. Ordinarily, she would've lashed out again, but his tone had changed. This time, instead of the sharp, biting monotone he usually struck at her with, it had changed to a more vulnerable response of a man rebuked for his hubris.

"We aren't engaged yet. . . because we're waiting for. . ." she trailed off before unwillingly leaving the end of her sentence hanging.

"I see," Sly answered cryptically, his condescension returning. They both stood there in awkward silence before Sly spoke again. "Good for you. It sounds like you're going to get everything you ever wanted."

"Yes," was all she could muster, and weakly at that. "Thank you."

The two returned to their uncomfortable silence as Sly turned completely to the bar and ordered another drink, this time whispering with the bartender. A minute ago Bridget would've given anything to hear what they were talking about, but now, she was too preoccupied with her own thoughts. Bridget's mind was swimming for what felt like hours—even that it surely hadn't even been a minute—when she realized that she should leave now. Just as she was about to get up and leave, however, Sly managed to change her mind.

"What's he like?"

She was not expecting that question, or anything further at all, really. She had to try and cut through the barrage of thoughts in her mind to summon an answer for Sly.

"He's, he's really great," she started, trying to muster emotion to match her words. "We're really happy together, we've lived together for over a year and a half, we've got a nice place in downtown. It's so great to have someone to love the way Ryan and I love each other." As she gathered her thoughts she started to gain momentum. She brought up their last date, but realized quickly that wasn't great story material, so she recalled their date before that, way back in July, when they had a picnic in St. Francis on the lake, but as she told it, it didn't sound that fun. Then she had to scramble to find another date story, so switched gears to an anecdote from over a month ago when they were out trying to rent a movie and how they realized they left both their wallets at home, which she realized was far less entertaining in hindsight. At this point she was having difficulty coming up with specific examples of cool or fun things they had done, and she could feel herself rambling. But she was determined to prove to Sly that she was happy with *her* special someone. Progressively she found herself reaching further and further into her past with Ryan to find anything interesting, until, eventually, she found herself telling a story from one of the first weekends after they had moved in together.

In that moment she had the terrifying thought she had at the end of the work day reared its head again, but this time not as a question, as a statement: she and Ryan *were* boring. They were a boring, lame couple, just like all her married friends with their babies. They had not had a true sense of adventure in their relationship in so long, and that fact had just shattered her shield of ignorance. She realized she had stopped talking so decided to wrap it up.

"Everything is. . . everything has just been really great for us." That last sentence was a lie, and she couldn't remember the last time she had told so many blatant lies to someone. Her world was spinning. She and Ryan were a lame couple. They were lame. When had this happened? She was twenty-seven, not forty-seven, why were they like this?

Progressively more terrifying questions arose in her head now. Was this a new development, or had they always been this way? Did other people say they were lame behind their backs? Then another terrifying thought: did other people look at her and Ryan the way she and Liz looked at Marissa and Jeremy?

Bridget took a long drink from her glass to try and calm her racing mind.

"He sounds like a special guy," Sly affirmed, the slightest trace of condescension in his voice. "You must be very happy together."

Bridget felt Sly's words cut her straight to the core like an icy knife. Her rapid-fire thoughts had, mercifully, come to an abrupt halt, but now she was beginning to feel sad and lonely. Again, while his words would've normally triggered her, this time, it sucked the wind out of her.

In her despondency, all she could answer with was, in a whisper, "Yeah."

Sly was in the middle of a long drink of his beer when he paused ever-so-slightly at her nearly inaudible mutter. Bridget felt herself slump into her chair, suddenly wishing she was at home in her bed in her comfiest pajamas.

But Sly said something that perked her up. Putting his drink down, he uttered, "He must've forgotten how to treat a lady."

Bridget wasn't sure how to feel about that. Should she defend Ryan from Sly's comment? Probably, but that would be admitting she was the reason they were boring. But if she agreed with Sly, then Ryan was at fault. Neither of those seemed true (and she desperately hoped it wasn't the first one). All she could do in the end was nod feebly.

She looked down, biting the inside of her lip as she did. She practically jumped, however, when she felt a hand on her back. She whipped around, almost expecting to see Ryan, she was granted a reprieve by the appearance of Liz.

"Hey, girl, you okay?" Liz asked. Liz had a grouchy look on her face that immediately disappeared after seeing the look on Bridget's face. Bridget mustered the happiest face she could.

"Just a little stomach ache. I probably need to eat something," Bridget lied.

Liz nodded. "Well we're getting a ride back to Marissa's place. Do you want to come with us? We can get food after we get there."

Bridget nodded. She took a deep breath and closed her eyes, gathering up the focus to turn and say goodbye to Sly. But he was gone! Just like last time, he was gone, disappeared! She whipped her head around, trying to find him in the thinned-out crowd, but he had decisively just disappeared into thin air again. How did he do this, she wondered?

"Bridg?" Liz asked, her concern apparent.

"Yeah, yeah, I'm coming," she said as she gave up her search in utter perplexity. Then she put her hand on her stomach, remembering she was supposed to be sick.

# CHAPTER 5

# The Fight

---

"Hello?" Bridget said as she arrived in her apartment. "Anybody home?" she called in the hopes that Ryan might've gotten home before her. The past few days he had gotten home before her, but his work hours were more flexible than hers were. Alas, today she had beaten him home.

"Ah!" she drew a sharp breath as she closed the door. She took off her mitten and nursed her finger. She had burnt it on the oven door yesterday, and had irritated it when she closed the door.

She walked into her deserted apartment, sucking her burnt finger. She hated being home alone. It made the apartment feel empty when it was just her small voice echoing through the high-ceiling hallways and hardwood living spaces. The echoes made it so eerie. She walked down the long hallway past the den and into the kitchen and living space. She kicked her shoes off and flopped onto her couch. What a day. What a week. While it was only the Wednesday after her latest night on Brady Street, it had felt like a month since then.

Work this week had been atrocious. Every day so far, the new manager, Tammy, had come after Bridget for something. Yesterday it was for doing personal things on company time, which was not the case at all. Tammy had just overheard Bridget checking in on an old customer and assumed it was a friend, which Bridget explained to Tammy. As usual, however, Tammy refused to admit she was wrong. She reminded Bridget that they were an *old* customer, not a current one, and that Bridget needed to be more productive with her time. Today, she had made some passive-aggressive remarks about Bridget's idea of "work appropriate attire," which was absurd, because Tammy had the same number of buttons undone on her blouse, and Tammy's skirt was even shorter and tighter than Bridget's. But because Tammy had to prove her power in her new position, today it was an issue. The only solace Bridget could find in all of this was that Tammy was treating everyone like this. Bridget grunted in frustration.

She tried to refocus on her work, but that had been difficult even without Tammy on her mind. Truth be told, Bridget had not been able to shake her fears from the past weekend. At this point, it was inescapable fact that her and Ryan were lame and boring. They hadn't gone on a date since Ryan had brought up possibly moving to Kansas. In fact, they hadn't left the apartment to do anything fun in weeks. There was no denying that for the past months—she shuddered at the thought of precisely how many—they had been a couple on cruise control, letting their history and chemistry carry them rather than building new bonds and new foundations for their relationship to grow.

Bridget hadn't been able to bring herself to tell Ryan her fears yet, mainly because she didn't want to admit them. The other reason holding her back was because she was sure Ryan would wave them off and say they weren't lame, they were just more mature. He was always saying things about how growing older didn't mean you stopped having fun, fun was just different. Bridget never really agreed with him when he said that, but the past couple of days, she was seriously considering that. She didn't want to admit Ryan was right about that, but her choices were either to admit they were lame, or that getting older made you lame by definition. Both sucked, but at least with the latter option, it wasn't really her fault. The one thing she hated to admit but could not contest, was that both points proved they were lame.

She had been trying to talk herself up by telling herself that just because the fact was inescapable didn't mean their situation was. She knew it would take work to change things, but they couldn't just sit around hoping things would get better. That was how they got to this point. Rather, for things to improve, they needed to *do* something. So for the first step, she decided she would tell Ryan she really wanted to have a good, long talk with him, one that they hadn't had in a long time. She needed to vent about how crappy work had gotten, and how upset she was that they were just going through the motions in their relationship. But most of all, she wanted to reaffirm to him that she still loved him and wanted to grow deeper in love with him; and for him to reciprocate that notion to her.

She laid on the couch in the dark for a considerable amount of time, the mid-November sun having been long set. Finally, Ryan arrived home, the lights off and Bridget still lying on the couch staring at the bare ceiling. He let the door slam behind him without a word, but Bridget, excited to see him, bolted up and rushed to hug him.

"Hey, dear," she said, using a nickname she hadn't used in a while.

"Hey, Bridg," he said, giving her a token hug before relinquishing himself from her grasp.

"How, how was work?" she asked, unsure of why he was rushing about so.

"Busy, things have been picking up lately. We've been getting some really big contracts, that's why I've gone in early so much this week." Ryan usually left for work earlier than Bridget, but she had noticed that he was gone before she was even up every day this week.

"Oh, well that's. . .," she began, unsure of how to finish. "I'll make dinner for us tonight. What should we have?"

"Uh, whatever you want," he called from the bedroom closet. "I'm gonna be out tonight."

Those words hit her like a truck. "What do you mean?" she wondered aloud.

"You remember, I mentioned, Jake was having a shindig tonight—the guy I best-manned his wedding back when you and I started dating? He just got a new job with a really nice firm down in Chicago, so he's moving at the end of the week."

Bridget, now very irritated at Ryan, replied, "Um, you told me it was happening, but you didn't tell me you were going."

"I thought it was implied," he called, still in the bedroom closet. "We're going to this nice place in the Third Ward."

Bridget was very taken aback. Ryan had mentioned it, but he had never said anything about going. In her frustration she refused to admit that this was her fault for not knowing. Besides, they never had plans after work anymore, so of course, the one night she really needed him not to have plans, he had gone and made plans.

"What time do you have to go?" she asked.

"As soon as I can."

"Could you stay with me for a bit?" she asked feebly.

"What's up?" he asked intuitively.

"I've had a-a really long day. And actually a really long week," she explained.

"Well, I should be back before nine. We can talk then if you're free. Jake and the guys are already on their way there, so I don't want to hold them up."

"I think, I think I'm going to be going to bed early tonight."

"Well, I can wake you up when I get home."

Wake her up when he got home? That comment triggered her. "Ryan. I really need to talk with you now."

"Is it about your day? Did something serious happen?"

"No," she said defiantly.

"Is it about your day?" he asked again, knowing that tone, his voice belaying his consternation.

She hesitated before answering. "Not necessarily."

"Well, I'm sorry, Bridg, but I can't talk now." He emerged from the bedroom in a more corporate casual look.

"Ryan," she began imploringly. "Please, I need someone to talk to right now."

"Well, can you call your mom?" he asked, sliding through the kitchen to grab a glass for water, clearly trying to keep the situation diffused.

Call her mom? Was he trying to piss her off?

He could tell his question had not been received well as he filled up his glass at the sink. "Listen, Bridg, you've gone out like five or six times since the last time I went out with the guys. Why can't I have this one? It's not even on a weekend."

"Because," she began with a mixture of pouting and frustration, "I need someone to talk to *now*."

"We can talk tonight or tomorrow, but I can't talk now, Bridg, I'm sorry." He took a drink of water. "Can you write all of it down? You used to do that a lot. You know it'll make you feel better."

"No, Ryan!" she exclaimed. "I need to talk to *you* right now!"

He stopped his drink and poured his half-full glass in the sink. "I'm sorry Bridget. I'll see you later tonight and we can talk then if you're still up." He turned to leave, but before he could, she gave a loud grunt of frustration and turned on her heel, rushing for the bedroom.

She felt her eyes getting warm as the door closed. A slight ray of optimism caused her to pause. She cried his name in the hope that he had overturned his decision and was going to stay for her. But, again, only her small voice down the long hallway to be heard by no one but her.

She started to cry softly, upset that her attempts to help their relationship had actually made things worse now that they had fought. She didn't know what to do, she didn't who to talk to. She couldn't just wait for Ryan, she would lose it if she was pent up here with her emotions. She didn't want to talk to her mom, who not only loved Ryan, but was always implying that they would such a happy *married* couple. She didn't want to talk to Steph or Kim or any of her friends, who would give her empty words of affirmation. She couldn't think of anyone who she could talk to about her confusion with her relationship that would give her real, blunt advice.

She stopped suddenly. 'Blunt advice?' her mind wondered. Actually, she might know someone who could give her blunt, real advice. Would it be any good, she didn't know. But it would be honest.

She sat up in her bed, and her mind seemed to slow down as she turned over this decision in her mind. Sly wasn't the person she really *wanted* to talk to, but he just might be the person she *needed* to talk to. Sure, he was kind of a dick, and condescending, but she didn't think he was a fraud; he had some real depth, she just knew he had to. After all, it was talking with him that started all of this, so maybe talking with him could help end all of this. Bridget tried to wave the thought away, but it had entrenched itself and persisted. What about Sly?

"But it's Wednesday," not realizing she had just said it aloud. It wasn't the weekend, how could she be certain he would be there? She couldn't be, but he did say he was there often. . .

She gritted her teeth for just a moment, then realized if she thought about it anymore, she wouldn't do it. She got up, rushed down the hallway, put on the first pair of shoes she could find and bolted out the door, on her way to Brady Street.

# CHAPTER 6

# Dreams

---

S he pulled up right in front of Mike's in a parking spot a delivery car from the sandwich shop next door had just vacated. She turned the car off and sat there for a moment. What was she doing? Why was she here? Did she really think Sly would help her? And if he would help her, would he even be here? These thoughts had dogged her the whole time, but she had kept them at bay by focusing solely on getting here.

There was a panhandler standing just outside the bar, but Bridget didn't even notice him as she walked as quickly as she could. She wrenched the door open more aggressively than she had intended to and looked around. Even for an early Wednesday evening the place was dead: one bartender and three guys on the stools, the music at a decided ambiance-level. She scanned the three guys on the bar stools and felt a wave of relief as she saw the third figure sitting farthest down the bar was Sly. She closed her eyes and gave a deep sigh.

He was here. At first that thought was a relief, but as it crossed her mind again, it became a question. He was here, why? Why was he always here? She dismissed the thought and reminded herself why she had come here. Walking briskly over to him, she saw him conversing with the same bartender as the last time she had been there, the same bartender as every other time. That was odd, too, she thought, that he was the only bartender she ever saw here. She ignored that thought as well, not having any energy or motivation to ponder that now. Approaching them, the bartender

39

turned to see her approaching, smiled, and whispered something to Sly. True to form, however, Sly didn't even turn his head.

"Hey," was all she could muster as she arrived next to him, refusing to take a seat.

"Hey back," he replied curtly, but actually turning to face her this time.

"Why are you always here?" she found herself blabbing the question. She wanted to slap her hands over her mouth. That was the question she was hoping to segue into after some conversation, but the cat was out of the bag now.

Sly gave the bartender a small nod, who gave an equally discreet nod back before walking to the other end of the bar. Sly let the silence between them linger for much longer than Bridget was comfortable with, but this time felt different somehow. Rather than Sly sitting in stoic, perhaps agitated silence, Bridget noticed he was tapping his finger slowly on the bar top, and his leg was shaking from bobbing his foot. Bridget studied these new habits of his until she realized she had forgotten her problems for a moment in doing so.

Then he turned fully towards her and looked her in the eye, something that he hadn't done yet; it made her take a small step back it was so unexpected. "Would you like to go for a walk?"

The question was complete a shock to Bridget. A walk? She had not expected that. In fact, that was the farthest thing from what she expected. She had fully anticipated a snarky, pointed answer, but she was instead rewarded with a question. And not just a question, an offer. He had never presented a side of him that could open himself up to rebuke until this. On top of that, he'd never turned to completely face her until this moment.

Meekly, Bridget began to nod until she could finally muster the only word she needed, "Yes."

Sly nodded himself, turned back to the bartender—who had been watching their interaction—nodded to him and said simply, "I'll be back."

Then he stood up. He was just as tall as Bridget had thought he was, maybe even taller. She could've worn the tallest heels she owned (or even Steph owned) and she still would not have been even able to see over his shoulder. He indicated toward the door and started walking, making sure that Bridget was in tow. They reached the door and he held it open for her as she re-entered the late November cold.

Outside Bridget let Sly take the lead, as he was the one who had offered. He turned west and started walking away from the lake. They walked in silence for perhaps a block or more. Bridget debated asking the question again, but she knew that he knew the ball was in his court. Finally, he spoke.

"I, uh," he began, "I know the bartender really well." Bridget had to remember her original question of why he was always there before she got back on the same page. "We've known each other for years and we're very good friends." She nodded and waited for him to proceed, but as the next block came and passed, she realized that was all he was going to say.

She asked a follow-up question, but instead of simply 'That's it?'—which was the predominant thought on her mind—she found just enough energy to ask a different, more meaningful question.

"You're always here, though, or, there I guess," she pointed her thumb back towards the bar, realizing it was several blocks behind them. "Don't you have more than just a nightlife? Don't you ever have somewhere to be?"

As Bridget was speaking, Sly did the most unexpected thing: he laughed. Not long, not hard, but decisively a laugh. Bridget wanted to ask what was so funny, but she was more struck by how odd it was than anything else.

He sighed deeply, cleared his throat, then answered, "Okay. I'll tell you the whole thing. But in order to get my answer, you need to tell me why you're here. I know you didn't show up here to have idle chit-chat or just to find out more about me. I can tell something's up with you."

Bridget was somewhat taken aback by the conditions of his answer. She didn't really want to lead off with herself, she wanted to pry and probe him a little bit, both to distance herself from her own emotion and also to ease the transition into her highly-charged situation. As she weighed her options, however, she realized that this was the only opportunity she'd get to talk to someone that night. Ryan was out, and while he said he'd be back before it got too late, he had a tendency to really let go in the off-hours if work was stressful. She checked her phone in her pocket, hopeful to see a text from Ryan saying he was coming home. But her phone screen had no notifications, just the background of the two of them kissing in the snow. That picture was from New Year's Eve, almost a year old, she realized. She hadn't bothered to change it. In fact, she hadn't even taken any new pictures to change it with.

She sighed, suddenly unsure if she wanted to talk at all. As she briefly weighed her options, another thought came to her, unattached to her own situation: why was Sly so secretive? Why did he always seem to have something to hide? There was no denying that up to this juncture he had been the strangest person she had ever met, but there was more to him, she could just feel it. And she had to find out what it was. Sure, maybe it was going to be a trap of some sort, like he would just tell some stupid high school or college story about how he and the bartender became friends, and he's just a loser, and that would be the grand reveal and the wheels would come off the traveling magic show.

But another voice told her to be at ease. It wasn't really her voice, but she knew it was coming from her own mind. It weirded her out a little bit, but it was a calm, quiet voice, one that made her feel at ease in spite of all the confusion in her mind.

"Okay," she replied at last. Out of the corner of her eye, she thought she saw Sly's shoulders drop a little bit. Was he nervous she wouldn't agree to his offer? She had to answer his question, however. "Uh, well, Ryan and I, uh. . . I wanted us to have a good talk tonight and just-just have a good night in, really have some good one-on-one time. But he had. . . something come up and he said he couldn't miss it, and I've had some work problems that I really wanted to talk to someone about."

Sly seemed unconvinced by her answer, his head cocked slightly to the side as he turned towards her. Bridget was unsure what to do, whether to try and shore up her story more, or just admit that it was a flimsy façade of what was actually on her mind.

"That seems almost as weak as my bartender excuse," he said with a hint of humor.

Again, she was caught off-guard by his response. Humor? And with sympathy? She knew then that she had to tell him everything. That was, after all, why she had come to him. Opening up to someone she barely knew seemed a better recourse than opening up to nobody at all. After all, if he proved to be a huge jerk, she could just leave and never see him again and all of this would be behind her. However, he seemed to legitimately want to hear her out. . .

"Okay," she sighed, gathering her thoughts. "Where to start?" she mused aloud.

"How about with the beginning?" he asked, again with a sense of humor.

Taken aback again, she regathered her thoughts and decided just to start talking and see what would happen.

"Okay, so, I guess Ryan and I are fighting right now. He's going out with his friends, but I really need to talk to him right now," she said, deliberately letting herself sound whiny.

"What do you need to talk to him about?"

She shrugged her shoulders. "I don't know. Everything, I guess. My job has really sucked the last two weeks to the point I want to quit, Ryan doesn't have time talk to me, and I just feel really alone right now." She didn't know what else to say. She wanted to get it all out of her, to get every last drop of her anxiety and stress out, but now that it came to it, she didn't want to share everything.

"What do you want?" he asked her suddenly. "Not from me, I mean, or even tonight. I mean, what are the things you want most in life?"

Bridget was very taken aback. What did she want? Who would ask a question like that to her problem?

"I don't know," she sighed. She didn't have the patience or focus to try to think it all out.

Sly nodded his head. "Well, then let's talk about what you have. You have a nice apartment, a relationship, a job, friends, a car. What isn't going right with all of this?"

Bridget wanted to say it was all going right, but she knew she would be lying. "I don't know," she repeated.

"So, all of it," Sly inferred.

"No," Bridget snapped at him. "My friends are good." 'Really,' she thought sarcastically to herself, 'that was how she was going to answer?'

"Do you like your apartment?" he asked. She nodded. "And your relationship?" She nodded again. "And your job?" She paused, then shook her head, then nodded her head.

"I don't know," she said, "I liked my job until I got a new supervisor."

"But do you like the *job*?" he asked incisively.

Bridget bobbed her head in thought. "Yes, I guess."

They turned off Brady Street and headed across the Van Buren Bridge.

"But you're upset about all this," Sly asked. The phrase seemed more a statement than a question.

She sighed and continued. "It doesn't feel the way it used to." Sly nodded knowingly. "I mean, my job used to be fun, but now I have a new manager who's really stupid and passive-aggressive. I really used to love my job, but since she took over, it's been awful. And I really love my apartment, especially when Ryan is home, but when I'm by myself—like today—it felt really big and empty. . . and scary. And I really love Ryan. . ." She stopped. She was about to add a 'but' to the end of that sentence, but had managed to cut herself off before she said something she regretted.

"I see," Sly replied quietly.

She wanted to ask him what he saw, but she decided to just let him have this one.

The two walked in silence, having crossed the bridge and entered the Brewers Hill neighborhood.

"What did you want when you were a kid?" Sly asked.

Bridget almost laughed to herself. "You're trying to be a shrink, asking about my childhood."

"No," Sly said authoritatively. "I have just one question about your childhood, that's it. What did you want? What did you want to do as a job, or where did you want to live, or did you want a family or what?"

Bridget refused to answer, she wouldn't empty herself before him like this.

"Why does my childhood matter?" she asked defensively.

Sly turned to look at her, but Bridget turned away just in time, staring at the sidewalk.

"Because our childhood is our age of innocence, the time when our rawest, purest desires are the only ones we have," Sly replied.

Bridget sighed in resignation. She decided to answer, but to keep her answers as short as possible.

"I don't know. I guess I wanted to be a teacher 'cause both my parents were."

"And did you want a family?" Sly asked.

"Yeah, I guess," she replied shortly.

"What about where you would live?" Sly prodded.

"In a house like my parents," she said, only partially true. "But the first time I came to the city, I wanted to live there."

Sly nodded silently to himself. "And do you have those things now?"

Bridget wanted to hit Sly. Of course she didn't, she didn't have any of those things. Sly gave her a look that indicated he wouldn't speak again until he got an answer.

Bridget stuttered for words. "I don't know. I mean, my mom worked and kept the house really nice, so I really admired her for that. My dad worked a lot, but he always said he liked his job. And he told me to find a job I would like as much as he did. And, I guess, my parents are still together, which is a not like a lot of my friend's parents—or even Ryan's parents, so I guess they loved each other, and I wanted that."

She paused as they turned down a side street. "I mean," she continued, "I guess I always wanted those things, what my parents have. But I don't know if I still do."

She felt memories of her youth wash over her, memories of pretending to be grown-ups with her friends, and playing house, and playing school. They were good memories, but also cold. They had never felt cold before, but then again, Bridget had never been prompted to really relive them.

Sly broke the peace. "You keep saying that you love something, like your apartment, your job, your friends. You do know that love is a two-way street?"

The question seemed oddly pointed, but Sly was no longer speaking so condescendingly, but almost openly, vulnerably.

"What do you mean?" Bridget asked.

"Love is a two-way street, the love has to go both ways. You can't love something that doesn't love you back. If you do, it's just liking it, or. . . something. But it's not love."

Bridget wasn't sure what to make of Sly's claim. She made no response, so Sly again broke the peace.

"You say your life doesn't feel the way you wanted it to, or think it should. You can see why you're unhappy."

Bridget huffed at him. "People change as they grow up. What we want changes. Part of growing up means giving up some of your dreams." She inhaled as she realized she had just uttered her least favorite quote of Ryan's.

Sly raised both his eyebrows at her. "I don't think you really believe that." Bridget felt like Sly saw right through her. "What do you really think?"

She took a deep breath, realizing now was not the time to lose her cool. "I mean, I don't know. I worked so hard for everything, my apartment, my job, my relationship, and now things are just so meaningless. I mean, Ryan and I have lived in this apartment for almost two years, we've been dating almost three years, I've had this job for five years and it didn't always feel like this. Things. . . things feel like they've changed. . . or I've changed."

"Maybe it's both," Sly said casually, his condescending tone returning.

Bridget wanted a sassy reply, but her wit seemed to abandon her, so she simply turned her head. As she turned, they cleared the thick brush on the side of the road and a broad view of downtown opened before her. She stopped, not having been here before, looking out across the cityscape.

"It's so beautiful," Bridget said reactively.

Sly smirked, looked at her, then the view as he leaned on the railing there, but he said nothing.

Bridget took in the beauty before her, her mind mercifully blank for a moment. But, much sooner than she had wanted, her situation returned to her. "Maybe it is both," she said at last.

"Why did you want to be a teacher?" Sly asked.

Bridget was taken aback at him asking this question again. "'Cause my parents were teachers," she reiterated.

Sly cocked his head to the side to show that wasn't going to cut it with him.

Bridget shook her head, turning back to the city. "I mean, I think I wanted to be a teacher growing up. I really loved playing school when I was younger, and both my parents were teachers." This time more memories came back to her, different ones. She remembered her pretending to be her mom or her dad, teaching her friends in a make-believe school. She smiled as she recalled dressing up in her mom's oversized high heels and strutting around the living room with a ruler in her hand as her friends sat on the floor and raised their hands.

But as quickly as the soft memory came, it left, leaving her with a shiver. She had abandoned that dream.

"Why didn't you pursue it?" Sly asked, seemingly reading her mind.

She remembered clearly why. "Well, mainly, teachers don't make a ton of money, and the job is really stressful, I know." Sly nodded. "I guess the biggest thing is I couldn't do the other things I wanted if I was a teacher. I've really wanted to live in the city and have a nice place. I wanted to do it myself, too, I didn't want someone else's money to pay for it."

"Like someone you love?" Sly asked.

Bridget gave him a small glare. "Like someone who didn't really love me." Sly raised his eyebrows, and Bridget knew he was going to poke and prod about her answer. Rather than wait for him, she took a deep breath and began.

"I had a rough relationship in high school—I know, high schoolers are stupid. But it was rough. I dated him all through high school, and he was really nice and sweet and funny. He said we could be together even though we were going to different colleges, and I believed him like an idiot." She felt her eyes getting warm. She hated recalling this. "It didn't take him a month to cheat on me. He pocket-dialed me at a party, and I heard him talking to some girl, then him just saying, 'Oh, shit, it's my girlfriend.' He tried to play it off, but when I talked to a mutual friend of ours, he seemed surprised that we were still together. It sucked, it was the worst. We had loved each other for years, and then he just went off with some random girl for a one-night stand." Sly shifted as she said that.

"After that I said I would take care of myself. The things I wanted, I would get for myself. My mom was married and worked and still kept the house clean, and I said I could do that, too. I said whatever I wanted, I would have to be able to do it and to afford it myself, I wouldn't need anyone's help to get it, especially someone who might hurt me. I wanted to be a teacher, I was in the education program at the time, but I knew if I became a teacher I wouldn't have the money or the time to do the things I wanted to. I decided to go for a different career."

Now that she said it out loud, it sounded very selfish and petty, but it was how she felt. Yet, somehow, even that reason seemed silly tonight, because she couldn't even figure out how she felt about talking about all of this to Sly.

"I don't know, maybe I should've wanted everything my parents have," Bridget, sighed, throwing her hands in the air. "I know how happy they are, and that's really what I wanted, happiness. My parents did it easy enough, so why can't I?" She was getting angry now. Why couldn't she be as happy as her parents? She had all the same things they had at her age except they had Bridget when her mom was twenty-eight. Twenty-eight. Bridget felt an odd feeling in her stomach. When her parents were essentially the same age she was now, not only were they happy with everything they hand and were doing, they had Bridget. This was the first time she had realized it. It staggered her.

She leaned onto the railing like Sly was, but more because she was weak from the thought. She looked up, but she didn't want to look at the city anymore. Wrapped up in her thoughts, she failed to see that Sly was looking at her intensely.

"You aren't the first person to ever ask that question, and you won't be the last," he answered cryptically.

She felt her temper spike. That was all he was going to say? Her hands had clenched to fists.

"That's all you have to say?" she asked him, her voice rising. "I came here for you to help me out, not just say things that sound really deep but actually don't help at all." She was getting furious with him. He sure knew how to ask questions, but he didn't seem to have any answers for all of this. What was he a college philosophy professor?

He smiled at her, Bridget getting even more irate as she saw how condescending he looked. "Well, I'm flattered that you came here to talk to me –"

"That's it, you're flattered?" Bridget cut him off. "Do you have anything useful to tell me, anything at all? Or are you just going to stand there and tease me and taunt me with your stupid questions?" She was ready to walk away right there, but she would give him one more chance, one last chance.

To Bridget's rising fury, Sly did nothing, no change in his face, his stance, or his stupid, arrogant lean. She wanted to hit him, to run at him and try to throw him over the railing.

"I know what it's like to be lost and confused," he stated simply, looking her right in the eye. "Because *I* am lost and confused."

# CHAPTER 7

# The Lie

---

**B**ridget gave pause to his claim, but she was in no mood to be sympathetic to his problems right now.

"Oh, what, did your bar buddies not meet you for pool one night and now you always hang out at Mike's, is that what happened?" she asked tauntingly.

"No!" he exclaimed with an intensity she hadn't heard before.

Bridget gave a triumphant smile and folded her arms. She had gotten to him.

"You have been lied to," Sly said plainly, ignoring Bridget. He stood up fully and faced her, but did not move any closer to her. "You've been lied to, and the worst part is, the person lying to you. . . was yourself."

Bridget threw her arms in the air. What an impossible man. She was ready to just leave again, but he spoke before she could leave.

"I think, deep down, you know. I think that the reason you came looking for me tonight—out of all the people you know—was because you wanted someone who wouldn't reaffirm that lie to you. You wanted someone to tell you the truth for once."

Bridget looked at him, unsure of how to feel. Sure, she had come looking for him because he wouldn't just give her fluff answers and tell her everything was great. Could what he was saying be true, though? He wasn't just telling her she was wrong, he was telling her that everything about her was wrong.

"When we're young," he continued, turning to look out over the cityscape, "we want things, simple things. Love, home, something to do, something to eat, to do what we want but also someone to pick us up when we fall. Our parents give us these, they guide and protect us. Life is simple because we are *given* the things we want. As we get older, we start to want different things. Fun, responsibility, independence, people to share our lives with, meaningful work. However, there comes a cost with all of it in that nothing is given to us anymore. We have to find work, a place to live, buy our own food, pick ourselves up when we are hurt or down on our luck. We have to go out and *get* what we want."

"Why did you want to be a teacher?" he asked her suddenly, turning back to her.

Bridget wasn't sure what to say. "What?"

"Why do you want to be a teacher?" he subtly rephrased. "I know why you want love and a home, those are basic human needs. And you saw how much your parents loved you and each other and how nice your house was and how well your mother kept it. But why do you want to be a teacher?"

Bridget wasn't sure of how to answer at all. She stalled for time by looking down and kicking her foot out. "I already said: because my parents were teachers." As she answered, however, she realized that Sly had baited her into saying that.

"Then why don't you want to get married? Your parents are married, but you don't want to be. Why do you want to be a teacher?" Sly cut back.

Bridget stared at Sly, suddenly afraid and curious. "How do you know I don't want to get married?"

Sly shook his head. "Really? All you talk about is how you don't want to be dependent on anyone else. I can see how. You got spurned by a lover, and you don't want that to happen again. Yet, you still want love. You want to be a strong, independent woman that can love on her own terms. On top of that, I know that you lied to me last time when you said you were getting married. I think you shouted that at me to justify something to yourself more so than to me. I mean, you don't have a ring, so how can you say that?"

Bridget fumbled for a response. "Well, just because I don't have a ring doesn't mean we aren't getting married."

"You overcompensated in your defense. You shouted it at me, then immediately apologized, and I know it wasn't because you shouted at me, it was because you lied to me."

Bridget had no choice but to admit that Sly had seen through her fallacy.

"So you don't know why you wanted to be a teacher," Sly stated bluntly. Bridget had no will to fight him on this. "That is the root of all of this."

"What?" Bridget asked, suddenly unsure if Sly had actually been listening to her. "How?"

Sly leaned back against the railing and turned to the city. He slowly shook his head. Bridget felt a chill run up her spine as she watched him warily.

"I can tell you why you want to be a teacher," he paused for dramatic effect. "It's because that is your purpose in life. You know it, or knew it at least, deep down. You can't explain it, because who can explain their life's purpose so easily in words? It can only be explained in feelings, deep inside you.

"You want three things, three things that I think most people want: a purpose in life, a home, and love. You had these for probably your whole life. You felt your parents' love for you, and you wanted it. You lived in your parents' home, and you wanted it. You saw your parents' purpose and meaning in life, and you wanted it. You weren't sure how to get it, but you'd know it when you found it. You grew old enough to chase those dreams, and you did, you had a plan. You were dating a guy, learning how to love. You were in school to become a teacher, learning your purpose. You were still in your parents' home, but you were learning what it would mean and be like to have your own home; and your own life.

"Then, something happened: tragedy. You were hurt pursuing the things you wanted most. You made yourself vulnerable, and someone took advantage of you. Then for your own protection, you threw up walls and swore off the things that led you to get hurt. You told yourself that if you became independent, you wouldn't need to be vulnerable. In doing that, you showed that you didn't realize two things. The first was that those things that had led you to get hurt were the same things that would ultimately heal you. Maybe not right away, maybe not before more hurt, but they would heal you, completely. So often the healing process is worse than the injury," Sly indicated her burnt finger. Bridget instinctively put her hand back in her pocket, unsure of how Sly had noticed that, but sure enough, it was hurting worse today than yesterday, even though she knew it was healing.

"The second thing that you didn't realize was that to want something at all was to be vulnerable. So this tragedy led you to a point where you had to choose between what would make you happy and what would keep you safe. You chose independence, to be safe, to insulate yourself from other people. That choice made you happy, because you expedited your healing process by closing yourself off. Deep down, however, you knew that it wouldn't keep you happy forever. But you had made a decision that you would not go back on, so you had to convince yourself that this would make you happy in the long run. You had to lie to yourself."

Sly bowed his head and closed his eyes.

"You've been living in this house built on sand for years now. A proverbial house—from you apartment, to your job, to getting married. They weren't exactly what you wanted, but you lied to yourself that they were what you wanted. After all, they were fine and they were going well. I'm sure throughout the years you've had moments where one of those things felt empty, but those moments weren't frequent enough to be a real problem." Bridget was reminded suddenly of her last date with Ryan, about how she felt like something was missing with them, how it made things feel hollow. . . empty.

"This house on sand, as long as there wasn't wind or rain, everything was good. As long as you never had any adversity with your life, you would be happy. But now there is a storm in your life, some adversity: your job. For the first time things aren't going well with it, and you're not sure that things will get better. That storm now threatens everything you've built. Your job has put you into a position where you suddenly aren't entirely happy with your relationship. And without a strong relationship, your apartment begins to feel unwelcoming. That means now you're questioning everything. You built a life that was completely dependent upon every part of it standing up, nothing could move or change. Now one part is threatening to fall, and it may bring down everything with it. Your house on sand is threatening to collapse."

Sly looked back up, but over the city still, not at Bridget.

"Ultimately, you're unhappy because these aren't the things you wanted, they're what *you told yourself* you wanted. You never stopped to ask if there was something better."

Bridget was stunned. How did he determine all this? She wanted—desperately wanted—to tell him it was all untrue, but the longer it sat with her, the more and more it seemed true.

"You compromised your dreams. And while compromise can be great for other things, the moment we compromise our dreams is the moment we compromise ourselves. That's when we give up any real hope at true happiness, and resign ourselves to our present condition. That's when we stop dreaming. Growing up doesn't mean having to give up our dreams, it means having to work that much harder to achieve them.

"Instead of a home, you settled for a nice apartment; but a home is not a place, it is a state of mind, it's shelter and peace. Instead of a purpose, you settled for a career; but a purpose is not money and promotion, it's doing something that is rewarding beyond anything material. Instead of love, you settled a relationship; but not every relationship is built on love. Love is a two-way street, both people in love have to give and receive it equally. You fooled yourself with these lies, and it worked. . . at least for a while."

He looked back out over the city.

"You gave up teaching because, as you said, then you couldn't have a nice apartment or be independent. I think, though, that you failed to consider something. You failed to consider that maybe, just maybe, being a teacher would fulfill you so much—give so much purpose to your life—that you might no longer need a nice apartment, or to live in the city, or to have someone to love. You never thought that you might feel more at home being a teacher than in a nice apartment. You never thought that teaching might make you happy in spite of not having as much money. You never thought that you might love teaching more than you would love a man. Because you never considered those facts, you poisoned your dreams. Our dreams are tied to our soul, they are the expression of our deepest, more innate desires. By poisoning your dreams, you poisoned your soul. And you've done that every day since you were betrayed by your first love."

Bridget felt her stomach drop. Everything she was hearing she wanted to say no to, to stop Sly from saying it, but she seemed rooted to the spot, unable to move, to speak, to think; she could only listen.

Sly hung his head. "You aren't so different from everyone else when it comes to chasing happiness. We don't *have* happiness, we *do* happiness. Having a nice apartment doesn't bring happiness, making it a home does. Having a job doesn't bring happiness, working towards our purpose does. Having someone to love doesn't bring happiness, actually loving them does. We *do* these things, not *have* these things. But the world tells us that having things makes us happy. But we have to stop listening to the world and start listening to that little voice inside of us instead. You probably heard that little voice telling you to come find me tonight."

She was stunned again. How did he know all this? He had to be psychic. Was she really that easy to read that this man—essentially a stranger—could know more about her than anyone else she knew? Suddenly, Bridget found herself caught on one thing he said.

"What do you mean, 'the world tells us?'" she asked.

Sly turned to her stared her right in the eyes. He seemed to mull if he should answer.

"The world," he chuckled to himself. Bridget looked at him as if he might be crazy all of the sudden. "The world," he reiterated, now dripping with sorrow.

"Over time, a lot of people slowly realize that they are unhappy, that their dreams have been poisoned and now their soul is sick. You aren't the first and you won't be the last. Unfortunately, there aren't soul doctors and soul hospitals, people to prescribe taking the hard medicine to the most rewarding end, to complete health and healing. Because of this, people forgo trying to cure this disease and instead deny that they are unhappy, they deny that there is a problem. They puff themselves up and tell everyone who will listen how great and amazing their lives are, how happy they are. They justify themselves.

"Thus the trap is set. When someone is telling you how great their life is, do you want to admit that you're not happy? Or do you want to tell them how great your life, too? All it takes is one person lying about how happy they are, that one person showing off their pictures and possessions and family—and then other unhappy people feel left out. Thus the trap is sprung. By forcing yourself into thinking your life is great, now you can't walk those comments back without even more embarrassment and humiliation.

"One person denies their own unhappiness, and then another does, both with the guise of complete happiness. Then people who see them join in the chorus, and it grows in volume and reach. More and more unhappy people add their voices of false happiness to the growing choir of liars, and then the next thing you know there are billions and billions of unhappy people who are telling all the world how happy they are, how great their lives are. In the midst of all of that, how can you be the one to say that you aren't happy?"

Sly paused, letting his words sink in with Bridget. A few moments of uncomfortable silence passed; uneasy, agitated moments for Bridget. Finally, Sly spoke again.

"That is how the world lies to us. Because if enough people proclaim a lie, it comes to be believed as the truth. You're not the first person to be led astray by the world and its lies and I can assure you that you won't be the last. A lot of people have been led astray, and. . ." he suddenly fell silent, his momentum suddenly grinding to halt, and Bridget waited on tenterhooks to hear what could have stopped Sly in his soliloquy.

"And I. . . was one of them."

# CHAPTER 8

# The Sickness of the Night

---

"I was one of them," he reiterated to a stunned Bridget. Bridget didn't know what to say. Here was Sly, this guy man who was always aloof and cold, opening up to her, admitting that he had fallen prey to the same mistakes she had. He had just deconstructed every part of her life, and now he seemed ready to do the same to himself. She suddenly hoped that he had a real story behind this, not something with his bar buddies as she still feared was actually the case.

"I was raised in a really small town about an hour from here," he explained. "I stayed in that town all of my childhood. I went to a high school the size of most people's graduating classes. Then I went to a small college surrounded by farmland and got finance and business degrees. Then, even to the shock of my own self, I applied for and got a job in Chicago. It was a really nice business firm, a global company, I would get a lot of travel opportunities. Like yourself, I was feeling the nagging emptiness of unfulfilled dreams, so I thought I'd chase them across the globe.

"I worked there for a few years and I got to travel to China, Vietnam, Germany, France, Russia, Brazil, Panama, all sorts of places. The job was very competitive, and I was working anywhere from forty-five to sixty-five hours a week just trying to stay ahead of the other people in my department. What I was doing was fulfilling work, even if it was demanding. The only downside was I was always an introvert. I didn't like dealing with people unless I could mentally prep for it. So when all my colleagues would go out for whatever reason, I generally stayed behind. In my free time I would often just read. Eventually, though, I learned how to socialize better—like a real person, and that unlocked a whole new career path for me. I became the best worker in my office.

"That got me a promotion and a transfer, as well as a hefty raise, so I took the job and moved here; I actually got a place not too far from Mike's, a place called the Starlight Apartments. It was an easy choice for me to take the job because it meant that I would actually be working fewer hours and getting paid more, as I would be in management. I figured that would allow me more time to go out and meet people. I was starting to feel very alone, especially because all the friends I made in Chicago felt more and more distant to me as I climbed the corporate ladder.

"I had never had a girlfriend, I hadn't even been on many dates. College had brought me out of my shell a little bit, but while I got first dates, I never got a second date. And now that I was making a lot of money as a corporate big shot in a new city in my late twenties, I said now was the time to put myself out there. So, I started going on dating apps, websites, going to social functions trying to meet people. It was still a lot of the same: lot of first dates, no second dates.

"Well, this had been going for almost a year. By this point I was compromising a bit with what I was looking for. I started just looking for anybody who would talk to me, really, and, I got some second and third dates, but it was with the wrong type of people. I didn't care at the time, I was just happy that someone seemed interested in me.

"Then I hit a lull where I couldn't get a date to save my life. I heard there was going to be a big shindig at work for the Fourth of July, a lot of people were going to go to Water Street to celebrate the holiday. So I went along with them hoping to meet somebody. It was an awful time, the worst place to try to meet someone."

He paused and Bridget allowed herself a small smile. Water Street was only fun if you were still in college.

He resumed, "If I could go back and tell myself what I was going to do to myself that night. . ." he paused, his voice heavy with regret. "I-I just wish I hadn't gone. Here I was with a bunch of people—I was technically their boss—watching them get drunk and make fools of themselves the entire night. It was a train wreck, I wanted to leave; but it was so grotesque, I couldn't look away. Finally, I had mustered the strength, I had had enough. As I went to pay off my tab, this gorgeous woman sits down next to me at the bar and says hello. I froze. Then she asked if I had just come from the office. I finally answered her, and the next thing I know we're talking and having a good laugh and a good time. One of my coworkers came over and started wing-manning for me. She and I, we kept talking for maybe an hour after that. Then when we hit a slow mark in the conversation, she said she had to get going and she was going to close out her tab. That's when a few coworkers started whispering to me that I had to pay for her tab and take her home. I had never done that before, and I was drunk on success, so I went for it.

"I paid for her tab, and I told her I could give her a ride home. She gave me a sensual look and thanked me. We got in the car and I didn't ask for directions and she didn't offer any. I drove her back to my place and we went up to my room. It was a small studio, I think smaller than she was anticipating from how I had described my job. But I grabbed a bottle of nice wine I had and poured her a glass. We each had several."

Sly fell silent, and Bridget could feel that it was an emotional part. As they stood on Brewers Hill looking over the city, for the first time Bridget raised her eyes to the sky and saw the moon was shining bright, illuminating the street despite the night. Faint traces of cloud slashed across the deep purple night sky.

"To be honest, I don't remember too much about it. It was my first time." He fell silent again. When he resumed, his voice was weak, almost cracking "At the time it felt like the greatest thing ever. I don't remember anything after that until I woke up that morning, alone. I had a terrible headache and no memory of her leaving or taking her anywhere, she was just gone. That wasn't even the most surprising part, the fact that my front door was still locked was. I thought she had stolen one of my keys, so immediately I went on a manhunt for main keys and my spare pair, both of which I found inside the apartment. Then I ran to the windows, all of which were still closed and locked. I was utterly baffled as to how she had gotten out.

"In all of the confusion of trying to figure out how she had left while locking the door without a key, I realized that I still had work that day. I tried to call ahead and tell the office I would be in late, but every time they answered they would just pretend they couldn't hear me. It was the strangest thing."

He paused again, the air heavy between him and Bridget. "I didn't know that the process was beginning."

Bridget almost blurted out 'What does that mean?' but held her tongue; he would get there.

"I got to work, and nobody said hello to me. I rushed straight for the secretary to figure out why she had been acting the way she was, but I when I stood there and tried talking to her, she ignored me just like she had on the phone. Then I started walking around trying to talk to people, eventually I started shouting at them but nobody would answer me. I even heard people right in front of me talking about me and asking where I was. I was furious. The closest I got to being acknowledged was when I stood right next to the two people talking about me and shouted in their ear. All I got for a response was one of them asked, 'Did you hear something?' I almost hit him right there.

"Then I went to my boss' office and walked right past the secretary and made sure to slam the door behind me. He jumped in his seat, but all he did after that was go to the door and look around before asking the secretary what that was about. Realizing he was in on this sick joke, too, I told him that I could sit there as long as it took for him to notice me. Well, I wound up sitting there for over an hour and he never even looked at me. I had passed from sheer rage to utter disbelief. Fed up with everything, I just went home.

"When I got home, I needed anything to distract me from my day, so I went back to trying to figure out how the girl from the previous night had managed to get out. I tried a few other things, but could not figure it out for the life of me. Exhausted, I made a simple dinner before going to bed early." He paused again, sorrow heavy in his voice. "I didn't realize it at the time, but that would be the last sunset I would witness, and that was six years ago."

Bridget's jaw dropped open. What did this all mean?

"I went to sleep on Thursday evening and woke up Friday evening. I was absolutely mystified as to what was going on. Frantically, I called work to explain that I wasn't feeling well and had slept almost twenty-four hours, but no one answered. I emailed them about an hour later and told them I would be out a few days on sick leave. After that I tried going back to sleep, but I had just slept a whole day away, there was no way I would be able to sleep. I wound up just staying busy throughout the night with whatever, reading, movies, TV, email—anything to distract me from all that was happening.

"Finally, I could see the sky changing colors from darker to lighter, but feeling no more tired than I had all night. I was planning to go for a run to get some fresh air, so I changed into some athletic clothes and walked over to the window. I watched the sky change from navy to indigo, and I'll never forget the feeling that came next. I blinked, and the next thing I knew It was night again. Just like that," he snapped his fingers.

Bridget gasped. No way, he was making this up.

"I freaked out. I was losing my mind, I was sure of it. I tried to trace back everything and I was certain it had something to do with that girl I had brought home. It was Friday night, maybe she was back at the same bar. Changing clothes again, I rushed off to Water Street to the same bar as two nights prior to try and find her. I spent the whole night searching the bar and Water Street itself, but I couldn't find her. Sunrise came, I blinked, and it was night again. I scoured Water Street again for her, but she was gone."

A pregnant pause hung between them. Bridget felt like nothing else in the city was happening or mattered, she was so entranced by his tale. "At that point the process was complete, the sickness had taken hold."

"The sickness?" Bridget couldn't help but interrupt.

He nodded. "I'm not sure how else to describe it. I mean, by that point I hadn't eaten, drank, slept, shaved or gone to the bathroom at all in two days. Besides the feeling of mild panic, I was fine. My facial hair hadn't grown, my fingernails didn't seem to be growing. It took me about a week, but I slowly began to discover what was going on."

Bridget waited with baited breath.

"I was frozen in time, it seemed. And what was more, I could only live at night. From sundown to sunup I was a normal person, freed of the necessary bodily functions of eating, drinking, resting, etc. But as soon as morning came, I would blink into the next night."

Bridget said nothing, but she was sure her face was showing her stunned incredulity.

"I had no idea what to do. I mean, who would in that situation? What would you do? Hopelessly lost, I sent an email to work saying I was taking an indefinite leave of absence over a serious health concern. Then I went back to trying to find the girl who had done this to me. But after a week, I had nothing. By this point I had to determine if I was going to renew my lease for another year or not. I didn't, because if I couldn't work, how could I afford a place to live?"

Sly went quiet in emotional pensiveness. Bridget was almost overwhelmed by everything he had told her. It was unbelievable, and yet. . .

"I turned to darker habits after that. I started drinking myself through the nights, trying to numb the pain of the situation. But I couldn't really get drunk, so what was the point? I tried to capitalize on that, going to bars with college kids, getting in drinking contests, sometimes even for money. I won every time. But what good was drinking a bunch of college kids under the table, even if I made enough money to buy drinks for a week? Finally, I took to just watching people at the bars, seeing all the happy people that would be able to go home and have a life when the sun came up.

"It was really funny," Sly chuckled, much to the surprise of Bridget, "in the cruelest form of irony, to hear people complain about how they would have to go back to work the next day, and yet here I was willing to trade anything to be able to have that problem."

Bridget suddenly felt very self-conscious.

"Then, one night towards the end of September, my lease almost finished, I was sitting at a bar on Old World Third thinking about what I was going to do with my possessions when a very pretty girl came up to me and started chatting. It was eerily similar to the way things had gone with the girl who did this to me. But by this point I had learned how to play those flirty games with women, and we bantered for some time. But then she said something that I was unprepared for, yet answered without thinking. She said, 'I live like there's no tomorrow,' and I said 'That's my life.' 'Oh, really?' she asked me. I nodded and she said the same. I told her she didn't understand, she said the same, we had a short argument that ended in an amazing revelation: we both had the same condition.

"After that we started talking about it. She told me about her experience thus far. It had been almost a year for her, and to that point she had met two other people like us. She also told me an amazing revelation: that as long as we were seen, heard, or felt, we could live in the daylight. But if not, we merely blinked into the next night."

Sly bowed his head again.

"I was so happy to know I wasn't alone. I told her I had an apartment, so I took her back to my place and we made love. It was glorious. We stayed with each other until morning, when we agreed to blink into the next night. We didn't want to have to worry with needing to see, hold, or hear the other person, we just wanted to pretend that we were normal people, seeing each other at night. The next night we gallivanted across the city together, knowing that now we were not so alone. Then we returned home. We repeated this pattern for a few nights. I had never felt more alive. I felt like this all had meaning now.

"Then, after five or six nights of this, she said she was leaving. I asked what she meant. She said that she had to go. I asked why, where could she go? We had something beautiful between us, something we could build a life around. And I will never, never forget what she told me after I said that. She said to me, 'We can't build a life together. All we have is a nightlife. What can we build with that?' I was stunned. I said we could build something together, we had each other. She told me no, it wouldn't work. And then she left. I never saw her again."

Sly took a deep breath. He had been talking for a long time and Bridget was captivated. His story was the most incredible thing she had ever heard, and it was clear that he still had much more to tell.

"Her words rung in my ears for weeks after that," Sly continued. "I asked myself over and over again if she could be right. But there was no way, I couldn't believe that, that would be total despair. Night after night, though, was the same, her words slowly seeming more and more true. Finally, they got the better of me and I decided that I had to embrace a nightlife.

"I started going to bars with the intent of wooing women, of seeking simple pleasure, pleasure for me only, with no regard to the fact I would do this to others. I would do the same things these two women I had met were doing, luring more people into this sickness, this nightlife." He paused, his voice heavy with regret. "I found someone after a few nights. She was a short woman with quite a body, very sweet, but definitely a pistol. I played her like the fiddle. She wanted it, and so did I. She offered to take me back to her place, I said yes.

"We got to her place and I pulled her close. We were kissing and fell on the bed when she suddenly pushed me off and cried, 'Wait!' Fearful of what she might say next, I froze. Then she winked at me and slid off the bed. I was extremely nervous as I waited to see what she was going to do next. To my infinite surprise, she pulled out several coils of rope and placed them on the bed with a smile. 'Tie me up,' she said. I was shocked at the request, but she turned around and put her hands behind her back. Unsure of what else to do, I started tying her hands together. But as I started binding her, reality broke through: what was I doing? What the hell was I doing? Here I was like a thief, about to tie up another human being and rob her of everything:

her dreams, her ambitions, her future, her life. I was about to do the worst thing possible to another human being, but it was disguised as the most pleasurable. I realized just how deplorable a thing I was about to do to her. Just how terrible a person I was.

"I stopped, took a step back and dropped the ends of the rope. 'I'm sorry,' I said. 'I can't do this.' But she didn't seem to get the point as she wiggled out of the ropes and kissed me. I felt disgusted by it, by what I had almost done. Then she whispered, 'I have handcuffs.' 'I can't do this,' I reiterated, but she failed to understand again and reached under the bed again saying, 'It's okay, I can cuff myself.' 'I'm sorry,' was all I could bring myself to say by that point. 'Fine,' she said, 'we can do it without them.' She turned away from me and started placing the rope and handcuffs back under the bed. I just remember wishing more than anything that I could disappear. I closed my eyes, wondering how I would ever get out of there.

"When I opened my eyes, I suddenly found the room dark and empty. I wondered what on Earth had happened. How was this possible? I checked the date, it was the next night! She was gone and the apartment was empty. I snuck out of her place and wondered in amazement what had happened. I learned that night that I had to ability to disappear at will, pending the same conditions as daylight: unseen, unheard, unfelt.

"I spent the rest of that night contemplating my actions, and in fear of just how close I had come to ruining another person's life. It was sickening, it was disgusting. I was appalled at myself." Sly chuckled suddenly. "How cruel it was that she had wanted pleasure and all she would have received was agony. How ironic it was that in trying to live her wildest fantasy she had inadvertently saved herself from living her worst nightmare. Life can be both cruel and ironic like that.

"After a few nights of living with that regret, I couldn't escape it any longer." He paused again. "I determined that I no longer had a place in this world."

Bridget felt a shudder run down her spine.

"There was no way out for me, no way to escape my condition. I was trapped, ruined, abandoned, and now I had almost done the same to someone else. All disguised as love. It was time for me to go, there was nothing left for me anymore."

Sly paused again.

"I made sure my accounts were all in order because I would not leave anyone in a lurch because of my death, I made certain of that. Then, I went to the top of the 794 bridge. I went there with every intention of jumping off that night. But the sunrise was coming, I could see that deep blue and purple sky yielding to the colors of the dawn, the pale indigo and yellow. I remember just staring into the coming sunrise. A few cars passed me, but no one bothered to stop. I wondered if they even saw me."

He paused yet again.

"I realized how beautiful the world was in that moment, how peaceful it would seem to those who could really live in it. But not for me; I was basically a ghost, a phantom. I decided to take one last look around at the world that I would be leaving. To my left I saw the million lights of the big city still shining in the coming morning, warm in sight, but cold in presence. Then I turned to my right to the darkness of the south shore, the coastline of trees and forest, the street lights and harbor lights illuminating the cold, dark water. Above the tree line I saw a single, solitary light peeking just above the branches. How had I never noticed this light before? And what was it? These questions piqued my curiosity, and as morning approached, I decided that I had one last adventure in me, one last night to live. I blinked and morning came and nightfall returned. That next night I decided I would discover what that light was, and that would be my last act in this world.

"I walked all the way to St. Francis to discover what that mysterious light could be. Sticking to the shoreline, I walked through parks and woods, even private yards, when I suddenly saw it again rising above the trees like a crown. Down a road lined with trees, old and grand, I saw the source of it on the hill there: it was a cupola of a dome. Walking down the beautiful maple-covered road I soon found out exactly what the building was: it was a seminary, St Francis Catholic Seminary. I checked the cornerstone, 1855. It was a beautiful building of a bygone era, even in the night it was impressive. I turned around back toward the lake and through the woods I saw the lights of the city, glimmering, but shielded in its entirety by the woods between us. Between the shimmering city and this domed building was a gulf of darkness, broken only by the streetlights of the road ahead.

"In that moment I felt a calmness take hold of me, the embrace of beauty and living poetry swept over me. Here, on this south shore of the city, was a building almost older than the city itself. It was host to a single, solitary beacon of light that was content to shine alone amidst all that happened in the ensuing century-and-a-half. It was unperturbed, at peace, and willing to be a bold contrast to the blinding lights that stood only a few miles away." Sly smiled to himself. "It had stood alone, only visible in the night for many, many years, and it still stood, alone and unafraid.

"Then I realized that I had to be just like this beacon of light. I had to embrace all of the beauty I saw in it if I were to shine a light to others. I had to stand as this light, apart from the rest, but a unique beacon in the night, in the darkness. A light can only shine in the darkness. And the darkness was all I had.

"With what remained of that fall, winter, and spring—it was early fall when this happened—I went to the public library, sneaking in during those dark evenings and hiding until they had closed up shop. I practically lived there for months. I read everything that seemed relevant, starting with inspirational works, then philosophy, wisdom, art, anything that could impart teaching and knowledge. I read so much for those months, and read and forgot more things in that time than I had learned in all the rest of the years combined.

"During this time, one of the big lessons I learned was to have faith and plan for success. I sold a lot of my possessions to gain more fluid assets, and then I invested practically all of my money, leaving a small fund for emergencies and nightly use. If I truly believed I could escape the night, I had to act like I would. I had to plan for the future I currently didn't have.

"But as the months wore on, I struggled more and more to hold onto hope. I was gaining wisdom and knowledge on a nightly basis, but not hope. I started spending more and more of my time researching my condition, trying to find anything at all like what I was enduring. There was nothing, not even a mention in the largest medical textbooks. No one had a cure. I had only a nightlife.

"By spring, I had tried reading religious and inspirational books, but I rarely finished those. They spoke so much of finding hope in the little things: job, family, chores, friends. But I had none of those things. What was the point? I finally made up my mind that the next book I tried would be my last book." He started nodding to himself. "I found a short book about a woman who lived in India who lived her life helping the sick—not curing them, just helping them live in their brokenness. It was different, so I committed to finishing the whole thing. I finished in a matter of hours. It was unbelievable, so I read it again." Was Sly smiling, Bridget wondered? "I found a quote, one that made me realize so much about the world and myself. It goes, 'If you love until it hurts, there can be no more hurt, only more love.'

"It was strange, and I had to read it over and over until I finally got the whole meaning of it. Then it was the most beautiful thing I had ever read. In that moment, I came to understand what love really was. I decided the time had come to leave my retreat and come back to the real world.

"I started going back to the bars, but not for fun though, or any of the reasons I had in the past. I avoided the loud, noisy bars, instead seeking out the quieter ones, bars with regular patrons. I started talking to people who came alone and drank alone, taking many nights to get to know them. I became a teacher of sorts, a doctor of the streets. I wanted to find those who could not find help in the traditional sense and see what I could do, because there was nothing traditional about me. This was how I could help, I reasoned. I wasn't making money so I could not give it, I couldn't volunteer at any charities or food pantries because they are only open during the day. The only places open consistently after nine were bars, the places where so many people with honest problems go to escape them. So, I went to meet the sick folks on their level. . . on my level."

Bridget suddenly realized how alike her situation was to what Sly was describing; she wished she could make herself smaller.

"I started meeting random people every night, hearing them out, listening to their stories. These are the people that sit quietly at the bar staring at their drink, sipping it slowly hoping that it will never end because when it does, their problems will come back. I knew that, because I had done the same thing only months before them.

"I met many people with a wide variety of problems—some simple, some significant. One thing I knew I could never do was compare my problems to someone else's. As soon as I did that, I betrayed the whole reason I was there." Bridget realized that of all the things Sly had said to her, he had never tried to diminish her problems. "All I could do was try to help them carry their load better. Sometimes I would offer advice, sometimes wisdom, but most often I found people just needed an open ear so they could air their grievances for themselves. Some of them even talked themselves into their solutions." He paused, with a trace of a smile on his face as he turned just a fraction toward Bridget. "Some just needed someone to tell them what they already knew." His face returned to its somber staring. "I learned that owning up and facing your fears was often enough to overcome them.

"Most people, after I talked to them, I never saw again. None of them ever sought me out again. Well, until tonight," he had another trace of a smile on his lips, and he gave a small sideways nod toward Bridget. Bridget had forgotten that anything existed beyond Sly's story.

Sly came to another pause. "I'm less helpful now than I used to be, and certainly less enthusiastic about it. The weight of years of toil without rest. My hope and my prayer has always been that some of those people faced up to their problems and overcame them. But each passing night, week, month, I wonder how much good am I really doing? The years of seeing all these different people coming to the same places with the same problems. The cycle doesn't change, only the names and faces.

"The thing that has really ground me down over the years is the fact that so many people care only about their own situations, their own problems. They don't have the vision or desire to see beyond them, to see into others' problems and situations. I know this," he took a measured breath, "because for how many times I've asked someone what's wrong with them, no one has bothered to ask the same to me. I've never once had someone to share my story with. . . At least, until tonight. And even then, you didn't really ask," Sly gave a sideways nod toward Bridget.

Now she wanted to be the one who could disappear. It was true, she hadn't actually asked him anything about his potential problems, she had only asked why he kept going to the same bar. She felt ashamed of herself; she was exactly the person Sly had just described.

Sly continued, "In a world where people don't care about other people's problems, it means they don't want to help others. And if someone doesn't want to help others, it makes them incapable of it. I've met so many people, and I will never know if they had the cure to my ailment, my disease, because no one has ever tried or offered to help me.

"I have one thought that gnaws at me constantly, my daily struggle. The thought that there is no escaping this, there is no cure, there's no absolution for this one mistake I made, there's no chance of change. That this is my life, my lot, and that there is no way to escape this endless nightlife."

# CHAPTER 9

# The Echo of Silence

---

Bridget and Sly remained there, silent, overlooking the shining, almost twinkling lights of the city from Brewers Hill, the chilly November air still. As Sly's tale began to settle with Bridget, she felt her eyes welling with tears. It was so much to take in, and so heavy that it nearly broke her heart. The only thing that caused her to pause was the thought that this was all a joke, a trick he played on women for their sympathy. But it was so outlandish, so disturbing, so dark, so clearly painful to him that this couldn't be true. She closed her eyes and tried to collect her thoughts as Sly continued to stare out into the night. She started to cry, not Sly's sake, but for her own, realizing just how small her problems must seem to him. And now to her, too.

"I," she heard her voice seem to echo quietly as if out of a great abyss, "I'm so sorry, Sly."

"Don't be," he answered with surprising rapidity. "You didn't do this to me, and you can't do anything to change it, so what do you have to be sorry for?"

She had no answer as the two continued to stand there, embraced in the echo of silence.

After a short eternity she realized how late it must be and checked her phone. It was well after midnight, almost bar-close.

"I can walk you back to your car," Sly said, noticing the time. She nodded silently and the two turned back toward Mike's on Brady.

The walk back to Mike's felt both shorter and longer than the walk to Brewers Hill. Bridget was in a state of numbness, a mix of shock and disbelief. She seemed to be floating more so than walking. When she finally caught sight of her car, her senses returned.

"Why," she began, her voice feeling very feeble in the cold night air, "why haven't you ever told anyone that before?"

"I have," he said simply, "but only to people who are like me."

"Why?" she asked. "If you knew no one would just offer you help for. . . for this, why didn't you ever ask for it?"

Sly answered slowly and patiently, clearly ready for that question. "Would you have believed me if I had just told you? Would you have believed me if I would've just asked for help?"

Bridget took a long, hard look at herself when he asked that. She immediately knew the answer, but she searched for any reason for that answer to be wrong. But she could not find even one.

"No," she whispered, hoping he wouldn't hear. He proved that he did hear it, though, by nodding slowly. Sly walked out into the road and went over to the driver-side of her car to open the door for her; she followed him, almost against her will. She felt aimless, her mind completely inundated with raw emotion, and so many different emotions at that. She unlocked the car and he opened the door for her so she could get in. She felt that just getting in and leaving would not do justice to what they had just shared with each other, but she could think of no appropriate way to say farewell. She got in the car.

"Good night," he said as he was about to close her door.

"Wait!" she suddenly exclaimed, thrusting her arm out to stop him. Her brain had suddenly recalled why she had come there and her original question which set all of this off. "You never answered my question."

Sly looked at her in utter confusion. "What?"

"You never answered my question," she reiterated, putting her arm down. "Why are you always here, at the same bar?"

Sly paused before his answer and said simply, "Because I know the bartender well." Then he swiftly closed the door before she could stop him and walked out of the view of her or her car mirrors. As she whipped her head around, she realized that he had disappeared into the night. Defeated, she started the car. Then she remembered that Ryan had gone out, and she checked her phone, hoping to see something from him. As she reached into her pocket, she remembered she had checked it back on the hill, and there were no notifications. She took it out and checked it anyway, hoping against hope. Again, however, there was nothing. She felt her emotions rising in her again, but she did not have the strength to decipher them, and began the drive home, driving slower than she had ever driven in her life.

She arrived minutes later to a dark apartment. She saw the bedroom door open, and a pair of men's shoes on the floor. She walked silently to the doorway and saw Ryan fast asleep on the bed—not in it—and his clothes from when he left still on.

She suddenly felt angry as she looked out the window into the night. She couldn't really explain it, other than maybe frustration from the entire night: at Ryan, at Sly, at herself, just everything. She stood there, grinding her teeth, as she continued to stare out across the night cityscape. Her mood softened as she continued to stare. When was the last time she had just looked out of her windows across the city, these floor-to-ceiling windows? Then she realized that this was the very same view she had looked upon from Brewers Hill, but with a different perspective now. She pondered that thought for a moment

Suddenly, Ryan snapped her out of her meditations with a great snort as he rolled over in his sleep. The thought flashed through her mind to wake him up, talk with him about everything. He did, she recalled, say he would talk to her when he got back to their place. She kept the thought for a moment, then realized that would require her to tell him everything that she had seen and had happened that night. On top of that, what would he really offer her? She couldn't bring herself to do that, not at this hour.

Ryan suddenly began to snore. Bridget rolled her eyes; Ryan only ever snored after he had been drinking. She kicked her shoes off and climbed into bed, debating if she should make a fuss of it just to wake him up, but as soon as her body felt the warm embrace of the pillow and her sheets, her emotion gave way to much-needed and much-desired sleep.

# CHAPTER 10

# The Decision

---

Thanksgiving came and went for Bridget and Ryan, and Christmas was hot on its heels. But before December 25th came, there was Ryan's birthday. In the days and weeks following Sly's revelation, Bridget had quickly realized that she had overreacted to a lot of things—not about him, but about her: her job, her relationship, her apartment, all the things she had talked about with him. She chalked them up to stress primarily, especially form work. There were, however, some things she just couldn't shake. The biggest one to her was that she and Ryan had become a lame couple. She had stopped trying to fight it and simply embraced it. In accepting it, she came to the conclusion that the root cause was they had lost a lot of the passion in their relationship.

She realized they had started just taking each other for granted. Ryan's off-the-cuff belief that Bridget would unquestioningly move with him to wherever he got a promotion was the perfect proof of that. Bridget still held to the belief that they were a great couple and meant for each other, but she was no longer naïve enough to believe that they could just get by without making an effort. As Sly put it, love was a verb, not a noun.

As for Sly's story, Bridget was still trying to absorb it all, even after weeks had passed. It was still so much to take in, and it was so heartbreaking. Those two reasons had been enough for her to try and distance herself from it. She noticed, however, that she found herself wondering less and less about if it were true or not, and wondering more and more if she had, unknowingly, met any other people like Sly. She started to wonder how many people like Sly there were in the world, how many had possibly hit on her or her friends on their nights out. Bridget made a note that if Kim ever tried going home with a guy, she would have to intervene.

As Christmas neared, however, Bridget found herself with less time to wonder about people trapped in the night and spent more time preparing for Ryan's birthday. She had started leaving little notes around the house that showed why she loved him, from his smile, to how he made her laugh, to all the fun they had together. So far he had found six, and she had hidden twelve around the house. On top of that, she had gotten him a wonderful gift, and it had come at no small expense to her. Almost since last Christmas, he had wanted a drone, and she was so pleased that she had finally gotten him to tell her exactly which one she wanted, but without being too obvious about it. She also had plans to take him to dinner at his favorite restaurant, a local favorite that could only be entered through a back-alley and was themed in Cold War-era espionage. And so far, the night was going splendidly.

"We're back!" Bridget said excitedly as they opened their apartment door, having just finished dinner, the drone having been gifted before dinner. Ryan had found another three notes, and while he still had two other ones to find, she had hidden the third one in a special place. "I have another special surprise for you." It was very small, but meaningful.

"Oh, do you?" Ryan schmoozed, leaning close and kissing her neck.

Bridget pretended she didn't notice, even if she felt a small chill of anticipation run down her spine. "It doesn't have anything to do with your drone, sorry."

"Oh, yeah," Ryan replied, standing back up fully. "How did you know that was the one I wanted?"

"You already asked me that," Bridget teased. "Don't worry about it. Are you ready for another surprise?" She winked at him and walked over to the countertop, rustling through a bag on the counter.

"Another one? You've already given me so many," he said as he approached her and embraced her from behind. He wrapped his arms around her and resumed kissing her neck before whipping her around away from the counter and kissing her passionately. After some time, he pulled away from her enough to see her and asked, "Does it have anything to do with this?" he ran his hands up her backside, all along her leather skirt.

"Every time you just have to say something about it," she winked as she turned back around toward the counter, this time grabbing the prize she sought out of the bag. "Ta da!" She had gone out just before Ryan got home from work and bought the new superhero movie that had just come out, *The Supers*. Ryan had gone to see it in theaters months ago not really knowing what it was about other than it was a superhero movie, but had come home from it and waxed endlessly about how it was his new favorite superhero movie and how different it was and how cool it was. His remarks had not gone unnoticed by Bridget.

"Oh, yes!" he said in genuine happiness. "This is awesome. I can't wait to see it with you. Can we watch it tomorrow night?"

"No, silly," she said, light-heartedly chastising him. He must be having a joke with her asking to see it tomorrow. "We can watch it tonight. It's your birthday, and I told you, I will only watch superhero movies with you when it's your birthday."

He walked over and embraced her again, nestling his nose and mouth where her neck and shoulder met. "Could I, just this once. . ." he started, leaving soft sweet kisses along the exposed parts of her neck and shoulder. She felt the ends of her ears stiffen in suspicion. ". . .get a rain check?" He seemed to whisper it before he kissed her neck gingerly again.

"For what?" she asked. He couldn't be serious right now.

"Well, babe," he started (she had talked to him about using nicknames again), "it's Friday night, you know, and I asked the bros if they wanted to meet up and go out tonight to celebrate."

"You didn't tell me that," she said, wiggling away from his embrace.

"Well, I did tell you we'd be hanging out this weekend," Ryan countered. "And you didn't tell me you had a surprise."

"Uh, yeah, that's how a surprise works. And you said this *weekend*, not the night of your birthday," she started forcefully. "You know I hate superhero movies, we've talked about this. If we don't watch it tonight, I'm not watching it with you."

"Bridg, please," he started, not whining, just imploring. "This is a great movie, one I know you'll enjoy. There's no costumes or nicknames or corny stuff like that. You'll really enjoy it if you watch it. It's so different than every other superhero movie."

"It's not the fact that it's a superhero movie," she stated aggressively, "it's the fact that I got it for *your birthday*, for us to spend the night together."

"Bridg, I really do want to see this movie with you tonight –"

"Then just do it," she stated bluntly, folding her arms.

"I told the guys they could be here at nine." Bridget looked at the clock and saw it was already 8:24. "Kevin even drove up from St. Louis." Bridget was unmoved. "Bridg, you fought me last time I wanted to go out. Are you gonna fight me every time I want to go out?"

"No!" she vehemently denied. "But you always pick the worst times to go out."

"My birthday? My birthday is the worst time to go out?" he asked, flabbergasted at her.

"That's not what I mean," she tried to fight, "I mean, I had a surprise for your birthday. I wanted to share this with you."

"Listen, Bridg," he walked over and embraced her, speaking quietly into her ear. "It's my birthday, I do like surprises. I'm surprised you wore this outfit, but I love it." He ran his hands along her sides and thighs. "Let's have a little fun now, and then maybe when I get back we can watch it, I won't be out late."

Bridget was unmoved by his appeals. "You always say that, but you never get home before bar close, even on week nights."

"It's my birthday," he finally said, decisively. He resumed forcefully, but not overbearing. "I'm going to do what I want, where I want, with whom I want. Okay? I had a great dinner, thank you so much." He leaned in to kiss her, but she turned from him and he had to settle for a kiss on her cheek. "I will see you later tonight."

With that he turned and walked down the long hallway to the door and left. Bridget stood there seething for a minute or two, furious that he would make other plans and leave her out of the loop. Then she went over to the coffee table and opened the bottle of red wine on the table she had placed for them to share while watching the movie; she doubted Ryan had even noticed it. Then she took a drink straight from the bottle. Then another. Ugh, what was she going to do with her night now? This was the only thing she had planned for all day. She had even braced herself for a superhero movie, which she really, really didn't like. They always had these morally perfect heroes that always saved the day, and the moral of the story was always the same. That, and they always looked really stupid with the costumes and nicknames.

At a loss for what else to do, she walked back to the counter and grabbed the movie. She examined it briefly, then opened it, revealing her last note she had written for him.

There, in the neatest, prettiest, most swirly font she could write with, was a heart-shaped note that read "I love you because of how much you love me."

She sighed to herself. She had specifically made this the last note. Here she was, going above and beyond anything she had ever done for his birthday before, and he was ruining it. He hadn't found all the notes, and seemed completely uninspired to find them all. She had even moved a couple to more obvious locations so he could find them. Then there was the fact she had worn his favorite outfit and pulled out all the stops to look really good that night. She hadn't done all that so he could go belly up to bars with his buddies from college.

She took the note out and left it on the counter, then closed the case, examining the cover again. This was the most frustrating one. They had made an agreement years ago that she would only watch a superhero movie with him on a special occasion. True to form, she had seen six, three for his birthday-s, two for promotions, and one when got back from a week-long trip to Taiwan for work and had gotten food poisoning on the flight back. All of this, and he had the gall to ask for a rain check.

She grunted and threw herself back on the couch, puzzling about what to do next. She wanted to put on one of her favorite shows and curl up with a blanket and wine, but she knew that wouldn't really make her feel better, because she would wind up staying up for Ryan, who would get home, tipsy and drowsy, and then he would go straight to bed. She also didn't want to just sit there and stew in her emotions. The only thing she could think of that sounded engaging was going out; she had, after all, put all this work into looking good. If Ryan wouldn't enjoy her like this, then she would at least enjoy herself. She knew all of her friends would be staying in tonight. It was frigidly cold and they were likely taking it easy in the buildup to Christmas.

Well, she wondered, maybe not *all* of her friends were staying in. . .

Sitting up, she looked broodingly towards the front hallway, staring at it as if looking for an answer. Then she made her decision. She stood up, grabbed her coat, and slid her heels back on. Looking herself over in the mirror to make sure she was still presentable, she suddenly debated changing. She knew Sly would have a smartass comment about her skirt, but she didn't care at this juncture. Zipping her coat up, she turned the lights off and left for Brady Street.

She parked her car on a side-street near Brady before getting out and heading directly to Mike's, very thankful that there was almost no snow on the ground to make parking difficult. She got to Mike's, opened the door, and was immediately surprised to see it was busier than the last Friday she had been there. She scanned the bar quickly, expecting to see Sly right away, but she didn't see him! She scanned again, but didn't find him. Where could he be? She noticed that a lot of the eyes in the dimly-lit bar were resting upon her. Feeling uncomfortable, she walked up to the bar and sat down.

Where could he be, she wondered? He said he was always here, where was he tonight? Did she scare him off last time? Was he somewhere else for once? Did some other girl bother him tonight to the point he would disappear into the next night, and now she wouldn't get to see him?

Her anxiety was beginning to escalate. Had everything just been a big joke after all? She looked around frantically again until she saw the same hipster bartender that was always here. He came over to her and asked if she wanted a drink. What she really wanted to ask him where Sly was, but she held back on that right away, not wanting to sound desperate. She simply ordered a drink instead. The bar was warmer than she was anticipating, so she took her coat off.

When he gave her drink to her, she asked, "Have you seen–" but she was cut off by a voice behind her.

"Thanks for the drink," came that clear, condescending monotone she had come to recognize. She turned and saw Sly sit down on the bar stool next to her.

"Hey, Sly," she said, more cheerily than she had anticipated.

"Hey, Foxy," he said in reply, ordering a drink of his own. She had to suppress a snort. At some point she would have to tell him her real name, but until then she would enjoy this little private joke.

"Where were you?" she asked.

"Bathroom."

"I thought you don't need to use the bathroom?" she asked, loud enough that he gave her a sharp look.

"I wasn't using it," he hissed. "I was checking it for JP. We've got an agreement that if I check it every hour, I get to drink for free."

"JP?" she asked.

The bartender served Sly his drink. "Thanks, JP," he said, looking at her out of the corner of his eye.

'Oh,' she mouthed to him.

"What brings you here tonight? I can tell you're not doing too hot, even though you're trying to look it." Here was the smartass comment she had been anticipating, but it wasn't quite as pointed as she thought it would be. It was even a bit—dare she think it—sympathetic.

"Well," she started. "It's Ryan's birthday today, and I had stuff planned for him. I gave him his gift, we went to dinner, then I had a surprise for him when he got home. I hate superhero movies and Ryan loves them, so I bought his favorite one, and we were going to watch it together. But when I surprised him with it, he said he was going out with his friends. We had a little fight and he left." As she finished the story she realized how mild, even childish it seemed.

"What makes it so bad," she continued abruptly, trying to hype it up a bit now, "is that I'm really trying to work on our relationship. I mean, you don't realize how hard I had to pry to find out just the right gift for him. He still hasn't even taken it out of the box. And then when we first started dating we made an agreement that I would only watch superhero movies on his birthday or special days. And then I left all these notes around the house for him that told him all these different reasons why I love him. I mean, I'm trying really hard to make him happy, but. . ." she trailed off. "I just really want our relationship to grow, I guess."

Sly answered in his traditional, patient manner. "Well, correct me if I'm wrong, but what exactly would growing your relationship look like? You live together, you eat together, you sleep together, you see each other every day. What more do you want?"

It was a hard question, Bridget realized. She wasn't sure what to say, especially because of how Sly had phrased it. "I guess," she started, "I want it all to feel different. To feel like it did when we first moved in together. I want more adventure. I mean, sure we eat together every night, but we don't really go on dates often. We live together but a lot of times it feels like we're just there at the same time. We see each other every day, but some days it feels like, I don't know, like we need a break—not like that," she quickly backpedaled, "but like we need to see other people—no, like other friends. I'm really screwing this up, I'm sorry." She went deathly silent, realizing the words she was saying even if she didn't mean how Sly might be taking them.

"I guess I don't know," she finally murmured.

"When was the last time you two said that you love each other –"

"Over dinner," Bridget answered quickly.

"I wasn't finished with my question," Sly said, clearly unhappy by Bridget's hasty answer. "When was the last time you two said that you love each other. . . *and meant it*? Really meant it, like that you would give up anything to have him and he, you? That one of you said it out of the blue, without an immediate reason." Bridget wanted to answer when she was writing Ryan's notes, but she hadn't really said it *to* Ryan. She had to think.

Before he gave her too much time to answer, however, he was on her again. "Or when was the last time you were somewhere by yourself and you thought to yourself how much you love him?"

She immediately thought of all the times she thought about Ryan at work; but that wasn't so much about how much she loved him, just how much she wanted to see him because it meant her work day was done. Bridget wondered and searched her memory for an answer to this question now. She had told Ryan that she loved him, but now those times always seemed off-handed, or more out of thankfulness for something. Like today, when Ryan was so pleased that she was taking him to his favorite restaurant that he leaned all the way over the table to kiss her.

Her mind moved to old memories. Memories about times in the past when they first moved in, how any moment could turn romantic. Memories about making dinner together, cleaning the apartment, even just going for a walk in their new neighborhood, how everything felt like an adventure. She had started a journal at that time about them as a couple. The bottom of her stomach dropped when she suddenly realized she couldn't remember the last time she had written something in it. But then, when was the last time something happened worthy enough to put in there?

Then she remembered for their one-year anniversary he had given her a jar that was full of 365 little slips of paper, some of them had date ideas, some had cute ice-breakers, some of them were just compliments about her. Oh, no! She hadn't opened that jar in forever! She suddenly remembered that it was sitting on her dresser, untouched for over a year. She felt terrible. Here she was getting mad at Ryan for not finding her twelve notes, while she had made it only halfway through 365 notes from him. She felt sick.

Sly sat in patient silence, slowly realizing that Bridget did not have an answer for him. He finished his drink, ordered another one, and then turned to Bridget and asked another question, decidedly pointed. "Why are you with him? Why are you *still* with him?"

Bridget quietly uttered a small, insincere answer through her cracking voice. "Because I love him."

Sly nodded with his eyes closed and turned his full attention back to the bar.

Bridget felt awful. She had come here for someone to talk to, not to be reminded how upset she already was. She decided to leave.

"I have to get going," she said simply.

"I understand," Sly said.

"Thanks for listening," Bridget said in an emotionless tone.

"You're welcome," Sly said, also standing up as Bridget did.

"Where are you going?" She started slipping into her coat, which Sly helped her with.

"To walk you to your car."

"I'll be fine," Bridget answered. She was more than a little surprised that the same guy who had literally disappeared to get away from the last three times they saw each other would now want to walk her to her car.

"No, I'm walking you there," he muttered back, waiting for her to zip up her coat.

"No, seriously, I'll be fine," she started, but she saw how intently he was staring at her; she decided to drop the issue.

The two exited the bar amidst a steady, December snowfall—light and airy, but very cold; the streets were lined in the white powder, and the sidewalk pavement was hidden by a thin blanket of white. Sly asked where her car was, and she started leading him. Then he told her that he was glad he was walking with her, it was further than he thought. She noticed he didn't have a jacket on, and he was starting to shiver and breathe into his hands.

"You need a coat," she said.

He shook his head. "I'm fine."

She suddenly hit a crack in the pavement, disguised by the snow and tripped. Instinctively, she reached out for Sly, who caught her smoothly.

"Thanks," she muttered, being sure to avoid eye-contact as she straightened up and continued walking. Sly said nothing.

The two arrived at her car, and he walked to the driver-side and opened the door for her. She realized this was the second time he had done this for her; she paused as she realized she couldn't remember the last time Ryan had opened her door for her. She walked around the door, then stopped, turned abruptly and gave him a hug.

"Thank you," she said, her arms around him, "for listening to me."

"It's not a big deal," Sly said, the two of them standing there somewhat awkwardly "I've listened to a lot of people, with stories way worse than yours."

Bridget wasn't sure how to respond, but she saw him starting to shiver. "You need a coat," she said decisively.

"I told you already, I'm fine." Was his tone rising, Bridget wondered?

"No, really," she said. "If you need me to, I'll be happy to go to the store and get you one. I know not many stores are open into the night."

"There's more than enough stores open into the night this time of year to get a jacket if I wanted one," Sly said, throwing his arms in the air to indicate that he was fine. His brief teeth-chattering, however, gave him away.

"You are so frustrating sometimes."

"You're so frustrating sometimes," he echoed childishly through chattering teeth.

"Ugh!" she cried in frustration, taking a big step backward. As she stepped, however, her heel caught a patch of ice, and she slipped, falling backward.

Sly reacted quickly, grabbing both her wrists and yanking her toward him. She bumped into him, her face hitting him square in the shoulder. As she did, she bit her lip.

"Ow, ow!" she cried.

"What?" Sly asked, letting go of her and bending over.

Bridget dabbed her lip with her finger, seeing the blood on her finger as he saw it on her lip.

"I'm sorry," Sly replied, staring at her lip for a moment.

Bridget rubbed it briefly. "It's okay," she replied. She pinched her bleeding lip with her other lip, which helped the pain a little bit. "This wouldn't have happened if you had a coat."

"Okay," he shook his head a bit to show his frustration now. Bridget gave a secret smile. "I'm fine. Really. I don't need a coat, I'm not cold-" Bridget could hear his teeth chattering "- and this would've happened whether I was here or not."

She balled her hands into fists. "You're so frustrating."

"I'm–" he started, but Bridget had heard enough. Her lip was hurting and she just wanted him to shut up.

She reached her hands up to the back of his neck and pulled his face towards hers, feeling his lips touching her. She felt his hands grab her waist, pause just a moment, then push her away. An instant too late, she realized what she had just done.

"I'm. . . I'm," she stuttered. What had made her decide to do that?

"Yeah," was all a stunned Sly could say.

"I should go," Bridget said uneasily.

"Yeah," Sly muttered again. He walked to the sidewalk as Bridget got in her car and turned the engine on. She backed out of her angle parking and into the street, all as if in a trance. As she shifted the car into drive, she looked out the window, expecting Sly to have disappeared. But he was still there, watching her leave. She wasn't sure whether to wave or not, so she simply drove away. As she reached the corner and turned, she looked back down the sidewalk and Sly still standing there, shivering.

# CHAPTER 11

# The Bartender

---

The next couple weeks were very introspective ones for Bridget. She had finally mustered the courage to grab Ryan in a down moment and tell him that they needed to talk. She explained all her troubles with him and her thoughts on the state of their relationship. Ryan paid attention and didn't try to fight her on anything. When she had finally said her part, however, he—predictably—downplayed a lot of her concerns. He said growing older and getting settled were probably the reasons she felt that way. They didn't stay young forever, after all. In addition, Ryan explained that when his work was super stressful, it made him see the flaws in everything else. Work was probably just grinding her down. Bridget admitted all of his reasons were legitimate, but they could not allow them to be excuses. In the end, he agreed with her that the two of them needed to refocus.

They made their joint resolution just before Christmas, and while it made Christmas a little strange, by New Year's Eve they had started to turn the ship around. They went to the casino with a lot of Ryan's work friends, a fair number of them single. They danced, they drank, they watched some of Ryan's friends make complete fools of themselves, and they stayed up together later than they had in months. Bridget had to admit, it was their best New Year's yet.

As January progressed into February, their relationship more and more appeared to be on the mend. They had gone on two dates since New Year's, were spending more time with their friends as a couple, and had even been trying to find ways to make their duller, quieter moments at home more engaging. Their relationship was fun again. Ryan had even found the other two notes Bridget had hidden for him, the one taking Ryan almost twenty minutes of legitimately searching to find it (she had re-hidden it just prior to his search behind a couch pillow that Ryan always moved when he sat on it). The last note, however—the one that she had initially hidden in the case of his favorite superhero movie (which she did not watch with him despite his pleading)—she had kept. Ryan hadn't known there were twelve, so he didn't know to ask. So Bridget had kept it to herself, for reasons even she didn't really know.

By this point, however, she had realized that despite their renewed relationship, something was still off: the spark hadn't returned. It was fun again, but it still wasn't like it had been when they had started dating. While Ryan was doing a lot of the things from their early days of dating—from nicknames, to trying to be more spontaneous, to having meaningful conversations more often—none of it felt authentically him. It seemed that he was using nicknames only because she asked him to, not because he wanted to; everything she was asking for seemed like that. He was trying, but his heart wasn't in it. She had concluded that he didn't like nicknames anymore, because never once in their conversation had he asked her to go back to using them for him.

All the same, it was the middle of February, the coldest time of the year, and their three-year anniversary was coming up in less than a week. They both had gotten excited about that. Ryan had called and gotten a reservation at one of the nicest restaurants in town and they had purposely only planned dinner and agreed to let the night take them wherever afterwards.

The big day finally came and Bridget actually had a decent day at work. Tammy was still the worst, but she had gotten over her power-complex and settled down a bit. That, and she seemed to dislike the new girl far more than Bridget. As Bridget got home she got a text from Steph and Kim and few others congratulating her on three years. They asked if she wanted to go out with them and celebrate that night. She thanked them but told them she and Ryan had plans all night.

Bridget showered and started getting ready. Ryan had said he was going to be home at 6:00, and she wanted to be mostly ready for when he arrived. But 6:00 came and went, turning into 6:15, and then 6:30. Bridget was getting concerned, but continued to get ready, purposefully going slower than she normally did and bustling about when possible. 6:30 turned to 6:45

and Bridget was decidedly finished getting ready. She grabbed her phone and called him; voicemail. Was he alright, she wondered, did something happen?

6:45 became 7:00 and her emotions had started to trump her rationality. She called him twice more, then texted him. Finally, at a few minutes past 7:00, he called her.

"Hey, Bridg, babe, I'm so sorry," he said almost panicked.

"What's going on?" Bridget asked, a little frightened.

"I'm so sorry, we just had the worst thing possible happen. One of the parts that we sell is completely faulty. We just recalled over 8 million units, and the team has to stay here and work late to fix this."

"You can't get away tonight?" she asked feebly.

"I'm sorry, but I can't. I actually can't, everyone is on mandatory overtime right now until this project is done. We probably won't leave here until midnight."

"Ryan, please, you have to come home. This is our anniversary."

"I know," he said longingly, a heavy pause following his words. "I would if I could. I really want to. But tonight I actually can't. I'm so sorry. I love you."

"I love you, too," she mumbled into the phone as Ryan hung up. This was terrible, one of the worst things that could've happened. All of hers and Ryan's plans for the night, gone. She suddenly wanted to go in her room and cry. Here she was, all dressed up, all ready to go out, looking her best, and yet, she felt her worst and had nowhere to go now.

She knew if she stayed here she would be a wreck. She had to get out of the apartment. Suddenly, she grabbed her phone and called Steph and told her she wanted to go out that night. Steph asked when and Bridget said as soon as possible.

About an hour later, the girls all arrived at her place; it wasn't quite the full crew, but enough to make plenty of noise. Bridge had changed from the really nice dress she had just bought for her and Ryan's anniversary dinner into more bar-appropriate apparel, including her favorite pair of heels.

They all had some celebratory shots upon arrival and put on some music. Talk was focused predominantly on how excited everyone was for Ryan and Bridget moving forward. Bridget told them about all the things they were doing to grow their relationship and all the girls found it inspiring. They told her how great she and Ryan were as a couple and how they seemed perfect for each other. At first Bridget reveled in it—she needed it after how uncertain she had been for the past few months. But it quickly grew from inspiring, to tiring, to irksome, to frustrating. Then came the questions that started to make her angry.

"So, when are you two gonna get married?" Steph asked flatly.

Bridget was not happy to hear that one. "I don't know, why?" she replied as tactfully as she could.

"I mean, c'mon, he's trying harder with you 'cause he wants to pop the question, obviously," Steph claimed.

"Whenever we feel like the time is right, I guess. And it isn't right yet."

Steph, however, was only the first of several voices that echoed the same question to her. Fed up with them, she made a point to pour the last of her bottle of vodka into her drink and then proclaimed they were out of booze and should head to the bars.

Surprisingly, there was a strong debate between Old World Third and Brady Street, which was resolved when Kim finally piped up and said a homeless guy had followed her to her car the last time they went to Old World Third. After the initial shock of that statement wore off, they all agreed they would take a ride-share there together.

Bridget had actually been in the Old World Third camp, hoping to avoid Brady Street. She still harbored regret for how the last trip had ended, but actually hadn't felt as bad about it as she maybe should have. After all, she had gotten home, Ryan hadn't been there, and she had gone to bed. The next morning, Ryan hadn't asked her any questions really, so she never brought it up. The fact that she hadn't brought it up, however, also made her a little regretful, but not as much as she felt she should regret it. The whole situation was confusing to her and a bad cycle of regretting that she wasn't regretting enough, so she had been blocking it out whenever possible. 'Besides,' she reasoned, 'she could probably find a way to avoid actually going to Mike's.'

The girls got in the ride-share van and Steph declared immediately, "Mike's on Brady."

Bridget felt the bottom of her stomach drop out. The other girls beat Bridget to the punch as to why go there, and Steph actually had some iron-clad reasons: there weren't a lot of homeless guys around to follow any of them around, they didn't have a lot of problems with stupid college kids or creepy guys, they could always get in as a group, and the place wasn't that bad. Bridget swallowed hard as the rest of the girls agreed with Steph and the ride-share headed for Mike's.

About fifteen minutes later, they arrived just in front of Mike's. Bridget was quite nervous and apprehensive to go inside, but none of the other girls seemed to notice, and Bridget allowed herself to be shepherded inside. Entering, they all found the place was busier than they had ever seen it, and—as a change of pace—the music was great. After their initial shock, the whole group went straight to the dance floor. To celebrate hers' and Ryan's anniversary, shots were purchased by one of the girls, and Steph even got Bridget a Long Island iced tea. With a little bit of booze, Bridget lightened up and decided to just go with the flow that night.

After that, Bridget had a great deal of fun. She was dancing, drinking, and just letting herself go for the first time in a while, which she desperately needed. She was trying, however, not to let herself go completely and get wasted. But every time she thought of Tammy, or Sly, or why her and Ryan weren't getting dinner together tonight, she allowed herself another drink. Before too long, she was feeling very thirsty for water. Finally stepping away from the dance floor, she went to the bar to grab some water.

To no surprise, the same bartender as always was working tonight. No wonder Sly was here all the time, so was. . . what was the bartender's name, again?

"I'll have a water," she said as he approached. "J. . .P. . ." she added slowly.

"Sure thing," he said in his casually smooth voice. She gave a short sigh; she had remembered correctly.

She wiped her forehead as she scanned the bar; she had been dancing more than she thought. The faces at the bar were all unrecognizable, except for—in his usual spot—was Sly, a beer in his hand. Whether it was the booze or something else, Bridget couldn't quite tell, but she felt an overwhelming desire to grab her water, go right up to him, and ask him why he did what he did last time, why he. . . No, she couldn't do that. Her rational side got the better of her, and she threw her water back, ordered something a little stronger than water, and headed back to the dance floor.

Another drink, however, coupled with the fact that Bridget hadn't really eaten since lunch meant she was feeling very carefree. A switch flipped in her brain, and she decided it was time to talk to him. She had to know why he had kissed her. She marched right up to him, no call for him, no smile, nothing.

"Why did you kiss me?" she fired away.

Sly turned to her slowly, stiffly. "Excuse me? Why did *I* kiss *you*?"

"Yeah, you heard me," Bridget shot back. He wouldn't get her with his barbed wit this time.

He was staring daggers at her. "Is that really how you remember it?"

"You didn't stop me," she said flatly. "If you really cared, you would've stopped me. You had your hands on my waist, but you waited to push me away. You're just as guilty."

He looked flabbergasted. "Can you hear yourself?"

She crossed her arms, the alcohol telling her not to give ground.

Sly threw his hands into the air, his long arms seeming like they stretched wall-to-wall. "Why didn't *I* stop *you*? Because I'm not the one celebrating a three-year anniversary tonight. With—might I add—only one of the people you've kissed in the last two months," Sly shot back.

Bridget wasn't prepared for this "How did you know it was my anniversary?" She couldn't remember ever telling him her anniversary.

Sly nodded towards her friends on the dance floor. "Despite how loud the music may sound, everyone can hear you and your friends over there perfectly fine," he answered pointedly.

"Oh," Bridget said, surprised and a little embarrassed. This had not gone the way she had planned.

After a short pause Sly spoke again. "Do you have a purpose for talking to me? Or are you just trying to make your single friends feel more lonely?"

"Hey!" she shot back. "Did you ever think that maybe I might be talking to you to make you feel less lonely?"

"Nice try," he turned away and took another drink.

"Do you ever just enjoy the moment?" she asked him.

He turned and squared her up. "Just enjoying the moment is how I got like this," he fumed at her.

She took a step back. She had never seen him like that. Somehow, him snapping seemed to stop some of the buzzing in her ears.

"I just," she started, suddenly sobering up. "It's been a weird night. Ryan is at work all night, and I had to get out of the house, and we came here, and you were here." She took a deep breath. "I'm sorry. You told me before that I should only apologize if it was my fault or if I could fix something. Well, I can't fix what happened last time we met, but it was my fault. And I'm sorry."

Sly seemed lost for words, for once. She enjoyed that part of the moment.

"Thanks," was all he said when he finally spoke. A silence fell over them despite the raucous atmosphere of the bar around them. Bridget debated leaving, but could feel that Sly wasn't finished yet. "Congratulations. Three years is... quite an achievement."

"Thank you," she replied. Then she sighed deeply and sunk a little deeper into her chair. "This isn't how I wanted tonight to go." Sly seemed to perk up a bit, but said nothing. "Ryan and I were supposed to get dinner at this really nice restaurant, but then somebody screwed something up at his work and now everyone is on mandatory overtime. It just really sucks. We had been going so well since Christmas."

"Christmas?" Sly asked.

Bridget dove headfirst into her story, telling Sly everything she and Ryan had discussed, all the changes they had made, the fun they had, everything. Well, everything except the note she had kept from him and sharing with Ryan the kiss she and Sly had shared.

When Bridget finished, she ordered a water because she was desperately thirsty.

As she did, another guy bellied up to the bar behind Sly. He looked over Sly's shoulder at Bridget and gave a low whistle. Then he suddenly clapped Sly on the back and muttered drunkenly, "Get it, bro." Then he staggered away.

Bridget wasn't sure what Sly was going to do, but he simply rolled his eyes.

"Do you know that guy?" she asked, mildly concerned.

Sly shook his head, raising his glass to his mouth, pausing just before he took a drink. "If I did, he would know this is a friend-zone thing."

Bridget overtly snorted. "A friend-zone thing? I haven't heard that term in years."

Sly seemed offended. "It's true. And real." he said simply.

"No, it's not," Bridget said, humored.

"Sure it is," he answered quietly.

Bridget was laughing silently. His lack of daytime interaction with people was shining through all of the sudden. "Look, it's not a real thing, it's just a place that guys make up as an excuse for poor charisma."

"Charisma?" Sly turned to her, looking mildly shocked. "That's not why." Sly refuted her point and she engaged him on it and the two began a hot debate. They discussed the friend-zone until they moved onto the things guys do that girls hate (believe in the friend-zone was one) and then shifted to things girls hate about guys and then unto all manner of topics from there. The two talked long into the evening. Finally, just before midnight, Bridget felt Steph grab her arm.

"Hey, we're gonna get going. You want to ride with us?"

"Uh," Bridget had to think for a second, but reached an answer swiftly. "No, it's cool, I'll get my own ride back."

Bridget second-guessed herself for a moment, and it seemed Steph did, too; Bridget reassured Steph she'd be fine and that she didn't want to go home if Ryan was going to be at work until after midnight. Steph nodded, an anxious look on her face, but said nothing. As soon as Steph and the girls had left, Bridget and Sly were deep into their conversation again, right where they had left off. They were talking, smiling, joking—Bridget even got a laugh out of Sly. It felt like only minutes had passed when JP appeared before them and said, "Last call."

"No thanks, JP," Sly said with a grin.

The two talked until JP said the bar was closed and they had to start heading home. It took some time, but finally even the drunkest fellows in the bar found their way to the door.

"Well, I should get going," Bridget said after JP closed the bar.

"Well, hold on," Sly said. "Hey, JP, is it cool if Foxy stays around?"

"That's fine by me," JP answered without even turning around. Bridget couldn't help but smile at being called Foxy; of all the nicknames Ryan had resumed using, Foxy was not one of them.

"Okay," Bridget said, halting their conversation with the intention of going a new direction. "I need a real answer this time. Are you always here only because you know the bartender well?"

Sly stared at Bridget for a bit, then turned towards the door where JP was latching it behind the last patron. "Yo, JP."

"What up?" JP asked, turning to Sly. The two stared at each other for a moment. "What?" he reiterated. Sly inclined his head forward a bit. It took another second or two before JP finally got it, a salty look on his face. "Oh."

"What?" Bridget asked in some alarm.

JP walked back to the other side of the bar, and the two looked first at Bridget, then each other, both with smirks on their faces.

"I'm always here," Sly began, "because I do know JP really well. We're very good buddies, and he's actually the bar owner, but he tries to keep that quiet." Bridget was about to respond with a fed-up response when Sly continued just in time, "*and. . .* we both have the same condition."

It took Bridget just a moment to grasp that statement, but when she did, she was floored. She did not see that coming at all. Then her mind turned to another avenue: was this a prank?

"What do you mean?" she asked, clearly flustered.

"I mean–" Sly started.

"We both have the sickness: neither of us can live in the daylight, we both disappear come morning," JP finished, a bored look on his face.

It seemed crazy, absurd, this had to be a prank by now. She had believed Sly when he had told her, but this was different, somehow. Yes, he had told her that other people had it, but that fact had never really meant anything to her until right now. She had seen Sly totally disappear enough to believe him, but JP. . .?

But then she started thinking about it. While she had never paid too close attention to him, his hair, his beard, all of that looked the same despite the course of weeks; like, the exact same. And now that she thought about it, he was always here tending the bar, too. Could it really be. . .?

"How did you guys find that out?" she asked. "About each other, that is."

"I was tending the bar here for a while," JP explained, his voice very monotone, "and I started seeing this guy coming in all the time, so I just started talking to him one night. We were talking about life and troubles and all the usual bar talk, and, I don't remember who said it first, but we both realized we both had the sickness."

"That's what JP calls it," Sly explained. "Sickness of the night."

"Better than calling it a 'condition' like you do. Makes it sound like a rash or a concussion or something," JP retorted.

"You and I can have different terms," Sly disputed. This seemed like an ongoing debate between them.

"Yeah, except it's just you, whereas I have twenty-five other people on my side," JP replied.

"Twenty-five other people?" Bridget asked. "What does that mean?" She had been bemused by their bickering for a bit, but that last remark bore significance she didn't grasp.

"You wanna tell her?" Sly asked after a short interlude.

"I gotta clean the bar, man," JP said, walking away. Sly took his customary patient pause before he started explaining.

"JP's been afflicted longer than I have," Sly explained. "By a good few years. He's six years older than me, too. Well he, uh, when he got his condition, he really struggled with it like I did. But he had something crazy happen to him."

"What?" Bridget asked after Sly paused a while. Then he turned to face JP and Bridget followed suit.

JP turned in interest of their silence. "Oh, what?" he asked, seemingly frustrated.

"Come on, man, tell the story," Sly exhorted.

"I gotta clean the bar before morning," JP explained.

"You and I both know you finish cleaning the bar well before morning rolls around. Just tell the story," Sly exhorted.

It was JP's turn to stare in discerning silence. "Fine," he admitted. He cleared his throat before he started.

"Yeah, I, uh, a few months after I found out about my condition I was really lost and unsure of what to do, so I tried meeting people. Here, there, and everywhere, just trying to find someone who might be able to help me. I thought about what someone in my condition might do. So, I started going to things like AA meetings, OD wings of hospitals, those sorts of places. And, one night, I was at the OD wing and I saw this woman there who seemed to be babbling about how she couldn't escape the night. Needless to say, I was interested. Well, the doctors of course chalked it up to partial insanity and permanent brain damage, but I stayed there until morning, talking with her. It was weird, telling her I knew what she was going through because I was going through it, too. Once she believed me, though we talked all night. She was perfectly normal, it's just no one would believe her about her condition. We talked until just before sunrise. There was a knock at the door, she turned away from me, and I blinked into the next night. There was another lady in the room, a psychiatrist. She was asking some questions to the woman. Neither of them saw me right away so I just watched and listened.

"The psychiatrist lady was explaining that she knew a number of people who claimed they couldn't escape the night and she left a card on the table and said they met every Thursday night, including that night. Well, when the lady got up to leave, I called to her and told her I was another person who couldn't escape the night. She didn't seem surprised to see me. She explained she was on her way there now and asked if I wanted to come along. I did. We got there, and I was stunned to see maybe a dozen people there. It was crazy." JP's voice started to drag and get heavy and Bridget realized he was having a lot of emotions welling up.

"It was. . . one of the most challenging things I'd ever done in my life, going to those meetings. At first I thought it would be a place where people would go to help each other and try to find our way out together. But I quickly found that was not the case. While the psychiatrist lady was trying to do something for us, ultimately, she was trying to help people that had something on par with a terminal, incurable illness. It was a very dark place. Most of the people there had tried to OD to escape their condition, and almost everyone else there had failed to OD and been found by this psychiatrist in the hospital. I was amazed at how many people there could be like us. I still am.

"But after a couple months I began to realize that I couldn't keep going. It wasn't a place of hope, despite the lady's best intentions. It was a place of despair, of desolation." JP fell into emotive silence again before he spoke. "A lot of people, maybe half the people I met in my two-month stretch of attending meetings, either just disappeared or committed suicide. The biggest problem was no one there could find a purpose to keep living, no one could see the point."

"How many people did you meet there?" Bridget asked, tears in her eyes.

"Maybe two dozen," JP said heavily. "The psychiatrist lady called it a 'sickness of the night,' which is why I use that term. I know there are more of us, many, many more of us. And not just because that lady found two dozen of us just in Milwaukee. I mean, I've seen people that I would bet my life on were like us.

"You meet a lot of people, a lot of types of people as a bartender," JP continued. "I've got a good grasp on the ones who share our condition. And I've gotten pretty good at picking out which ones are just trying to survive and which ones are bad eggs."

"How?" Bridget asked, beyond curious.

JP chewed on his tongue as he considered his answer. "Think of all the people you see when you go the bars at night. There are the career drunks, the young professionals letting loose, the college kids, the party wagon, the people that are only there because their friends dragged them there, the quiet ones, all sorts of people. I've found that the people like us," he indicated to Sly and himself, "tend to be in the drunks category or the quiet ones. Those people I try to talk to every once in a while, but they tend to shut me out, which usually confirms my belief. If you have a problem you can't solve, you tend not to want to talk about it, just drink it away.

"But there are some unsavory characters out there, too, people who get a kick out of ruining other people's lives. I've managed to save a few people from losing everything."

"How?" Bridget asked.

"I've owned this bar since my dad passed away and left it to me. At first I thought maybe trying to build a business would give me some purpose. Early on I tried to make this a happening place. Then I started to notice more people like us. People who look college or mid-to-late-twenties that are just a little too smooth with the ladies or the guys. You know, the ones that are 'in college' but don't give you any other details, and you only ever see at the bars. Those are people like us who are out to ruin other people's lives.

"Before too long, I realized just how many people like us there were, and if I get the feeling that one of them is here for no good, I toss them out."

"But won't they just go to another bar and try the same thing?" Bridget asked.

"They might. I can't control that. But I've made it my purpose here to stop others from becoming like us. That's how I've found some meaning and purpose for my life, by protecting the people I can. That was the real thing I picked up from those meetings, you need to have purpose to keep on going.

"See, the thing is, there's no awareness month for this, there's no public service announcements telling guys and girls not to go home with random, smooth strangers at the bar. In fact, it's the opposite, a lot of people encourage it. Look at this guy," he gave Sly a pat on the shoulder. "I've made it my purpose to stop other people from being like us. There's no cure for us, the only way to get rid of it is through attrition. If we, the old guard, can just die off without dragging anyone else down to our level. That's my hope and goal. And I know that's pretty dark, but that's as optimistic as I can be."

Bridget felt a knot in her stomach as he continued.

"I wish that no one else had to endure what we endure, because what we endure is worse than hell. It's limbo, almost as if we don't exist. We can't really live, all we can really do is die. That's what most of us do, I think. It's a dark, dark path we walk, constantly in the night, never seeing the sun. No one cares about us. No one. The one psychiatrist lady admitted to the group she was trying to get a paper published on us, but no one would believe her. No one would bother to investigate, either. She said she wouldn't stop until she got information about our sickness to the world, but that hasn't happened yet. Or if it has, it's gone completely unnoticed. Everyone probably thinks it's the ramblings of a bunch of brain-dead crack addicts. There's no road back for us."

JP finished up and after an exhausted pause, said he had to get back to cleaning up the bar. If Bridget was heartbroken after Sly's tale, she was in shell-shock after hearing JP's. True, Sly's had been dark, but it had just been himself and couple other loose cannons. But to hear that there were dozens, hundreds, maybe even thousands of people out there just in Milwaukee was arresting. Then to hear how truly sad and wretched they were; people without hope.

The three sat in an enduring silence, broken only by the clinking of bar glasses being removed. Bridget felt she had to say something to try and lighten the mood because the sorrow was quickly smothering her.

"What," she started, trying to get both of their attentions, "what do you miss the most about the day?"

JP and Sly looked at each other thoughtfully. They both nodded in deep concentration as they pondered their answers. JP spoke first.

"The sun. I miss the sun. I mean, I feel like a vampire just without the glitter. I haven't seen the sun in over a decade. Just an hour of pure sunshine and warmth, that would be paradise."

JP went back to cleaning the bar as Sly continued to ponder his answer. Finally, he spoke.

"The sunrise," he propositioned. They both heard JP make a small 'ah-ha,' in the background. "The sun would be great, and I miss it, don't get me wrong, but I haven't seen it in years, not even a glimpse. Like JP said, I've essentially forgotten what the sunshine looks like and feels like in real life. But the sunrise, well, JP just disappears as soon as his work is done every night so he doesn't stay up for it."

"No sense to," he called from the far end of the bar.

"But I do. Every morning that clouds don't guard the horizon over the lake, I start to see the colors change from black to navy and deep purple, to maroon and orange, to gold. And then when that gold hits I know my time is up, and I blink into the next night where it is dark and the sky is pitch. I haven't seen the sun or a sunset in years, but the sunrise, I almost catch that every morning. For once, I'd love to actually catch it, though."

Bridget felt a wave of sadness rush over her. Her questions were supposed to lighten the mood, not dampen it. Suddenly, a small but significant idea popped into her head. It was a bit crazy, and she had to make sure it would work.

"Hold on a second," she said to both of them, but Sly in particular. "As long as you're seen, heard, or felt, you won't disappear or blink or whatever into the next night, right?"

Sly and JP shrugged their shoulders at each other. "That's what I've been told," JP answered.

She bit her lip as she formed her question and turned to Sly.

"Would you like to watch the sunrise with me?"

# CHAPTER 12

# The First Sunrise

---

"I'm sorry, what?" Sly asked, seemingly unsure if he heard the question correctly.

"Would you like to see the sunrise with me," Bridget asked again, a bit more hesitation in her voice this time.

Sly turned and looked to JP; the two gave each other puzzled looks. Then Sly turned back to Bridget. "Sure, I guess. There's no guarantee it'll work."

"You two have never tried to stay up together and see the sun?" she asked in some surprise.

They both shook their head. JP answered, "We really aren't sure that it will even work."

"Right," Sly emphasized. "That's just what I've been told, I've never tried it."

"Oh," Bridget said, realizing that she might be committing to pulling an all-nighter just to prove an optimistic theory false.

"But I'm willing to try it," Sly spoke at last. "If you're still willing to despite that risk."

Bridget had to consider her answer with these new conditions. She really didn't want to be standing somewhere watching the sunrise alone in the cold. While it was decent weather for February, it was still quite chilly out and there was a fresh layer of powder snow on the ground. But this was an adventure, something she hadn't done in years.

After some careful thought, she agreed to try it with Sly. JP agreed to let them hang around the bar until they were ready to leave. Bridget and Sly stayed in the bar talking all through the morning hours. When JP had finished cleaning up, he then gave Sly a key and told him to lock the door behind him.

"You don't want to come?" Bridget asked him, shocked that he wouldn't want to see the sun after all they had talked about.

"If it works for you two, then we'll talk. I'm not the optimistic one here, he is," JP replied bluntly, pointing to Sly. Then he clocked out and walked into the backroom, bidding them a good morning as he did.

Bridget and Sly continued to talk about anything and everything until they could see the sky lightening. Since Bridget had taken a ride-share, they would have to walk to Veteran's Park, one of the best places in the city to catch the sunrise. Thankfully, it was just down the hill and across the pedestrian bridge.

She put on her coat and was surprised to see that Sly had a coat this time.

"It's JP's," he muttered as he put it on. Bridget smirked at him, but he pretended not to notice.

They braved the cold air and biting wind as they walked outside. Bridget felt a shock by how cold it was because of how warm the bar had been. Sly turned the key and tested the door, ensuring the door was locked, and they turned towards the lake.

They crossed two streets as the sky started to assume the hearty maroons and traces of orange Sly had described; then they started down the sharp hill to the lakefront. Bridget could tell it was a bit icy on the trail, and despite this being her favorite and most comfortable set of heels, they were still heels and she was still walking on ice. She thought about grabbing Sly's arm to help her, but before she could decide, she lost her balance on a thin patch of ice and slid.

"Whoa!" she cried as she reached out and secured herself to Sly's arm, who held her steady. "Sorry," she said after she got her balance.

"You should probably just hold onto me the whole way down," Sly said, somewhat begrudgingly. As she grabbed his arm, she had the frightening premonition of hitting an ice patch just as Sly would disappear. She shook that thought immediately.

She held his arm the rest of the winding path down and was happy that she did because the bridge over Lincoln Memorial Drive was especially icy. They had no more slipping instances as they walked in silence down the hill to the street level. By now the maroons were yielding to oranges and the oranges were yielding to the golds. They walked around the frozen lagoon in the park, seeing the icy vapors rising off the frozen body of water, admiring the wisps in the steady morning breeze as it seemed to twirl and wrap them into the heavens.

They walked along the winding trail until they reached the end of the road and there, before them, was their prize. The sun had just started to crest the horizon, and its course across the sky was uninhibited by any clouds; just the icy, wispy lake standing between them and the coming dawn. The sky was a radiant, pastel yellow, and all around the sun seemed to glow with a vibrancy that was absent past those few precious hours of the dawn. Across the snowy field, they watched and basked in the glorious revival of the day.

Bridget could feel the chill getting to her once they stopped walking, and even through Sly's thick workman's jacket, she could feel he was starting to chill as well. His shoulders were scrunched up to protect his neck from the nipping air and his breath poured out a cloud of vapor every time he exhaled.

"Are you cold?" she asked.

"I'm fine," he said stiffly.

"You are so frustrating," she said as she wrapped her arms around his midsection and moved her hands up and down on his back to generate warmth for him, hoping he would do the same. It took a bit, but eventually he reciprocated.

The two stood there for some time, watching the morning sun rise to assume its position as champion of the day. It climbed steadily as it shimmered over the great sea of ice between them and it.

"This is gorgeous," Sly said at last. "I, I haven't seen this in so long."

Bridget looked up at him, and while he still wore the same stoic expression as always, Bridget could tell that beneath it something had awoken, something had arisen just like the sun which inspired it.

"Neither have I," Bridget admitted at last. It was true, despite having full well the ability to watch the sunrise whenever she wanted to, she could not think of a time when she had gotten up early to see it, when she had foregone those precious hours of sleep she guarded so closely. It was a shame to be seeing this for the first time now. She had less than a mile to travel to witness this spectacle, this living canvas of art, which unfolded in a spectacular display every morning.

She nestled into Sly's coat. Her disappointment in herself was renewed by the realization that she had never once in her life gotten up early just to see the sunrise.

"This is," Sly exhaled, "just breathtaking."

Bridget smiled as she realized she had just done something for Sly that he could never do for himself. Not just that, but something he had wanted to do for years.

"It really is," she echoed.

They stood in frozen admiration for a few more minutes before Bridget started to get very chilled. She released Sly in an effort to indicate that she wished to leave, but he was entranced by the golden glow that was ascending the heavens. Finally, she had to remark about the cold to snap him back to reality. Sly then offered to call her a cab, but she said it would take just as long as walking at this hour of the morning; her apartment was less than a mile away.

"Then at least let me walk you home," Sly said. They started on their way towards downtown when all of a sudden Bridget's stomach rumbled loudly. They both shared a light-hearted laugh at that.

"I guess I haven't eaten in, oh gosh, like since lunch yesterday," she said.

"Wow," was all Sly said. "Are you hungry?"

"Yes," she said emphatically, and a little annoyed that he had to ask.

"We could get breakfast," Sly said precariously.

"Oh, yes!" she replied swiftly. "I know of this awesome breakfast place just near my apartment. We should go!"

"I won't eat anything, but sure," Sly said.

"When was the last time you ate anything?" she asked him.

"Phew," he exhaled, "years, at least. I used to eat the scraps of bar food at Mike's just to remember what food tastes like."

Bridget stuck her tongue out in disgust at that.

"What?" Sly chuckled. "I don't really get sick, like coughing-headache-sneezing sick. I haven't even had a stuffy nose since it happened. I think it comes with the condition."

"Well then it's not all bad," Bridget laughed.

"No, it is," Sly replied darkly.

The two fell silent as they kept going. Bridget clung to his arm as they walked.

"We're in dangerous territory," Sly said suddenly.

"I know, it's so icy here," Bridget said, her eyes on the ground.

"That's not what I mean," Sly said, a hint of grouchiness in his tone.

She looked up at him. "What do you mean?"

"I mean," he started, "it's the daytime now; morning. If you lose sight of me or let go of me or don't turn to face me when I call you, I'm going to disappear, and you'll be alone."

The harsh reality of his statement hit her all at once. "Oh," was all she could muster. They were, indeed, in dangerous territory. Her vision of slipping on the ice just as he disappeared returned.

"This is the latest I've been up since my last day in the sun," he marveled to her suddenly.

Bridget wanted to let him revel in the moment, but now that they had left the bar she had another question for him.

"You and JP," she started, "how did you two become as good of friends as you are?"

"What do you mean?" Sly asked.

"I mean, like, you two bicker and understand each other like an old married couple. How did you get that way? It couldn't just be years of friendship. Because I was never on that level with my best friends or roommates or anyone ever. Ryan and I aren't even like that."

Sly chuckled and looked at the ground. He was clearly out of his natural habitat, so he couldn't resort to just staring behind the bar to focus his thoughts.

"Well," he started, "it's true, we don't have too much in common. He and I operate very differently, as you can tell. I mean, really, the only thing we have in common is our condition. That's about it. But that, that alone has been enough to for us to forge a bond. We have a shared suffering. When the suffering is as bad as ours, I would say that makes us practically brothers."

"How?" she asked. That was the whole point, she wanted to know why that allowed them to forge a bond stronger and deeper than any she had ever achieved.

"Well," he started slowly, "have you ever read war memoirs, soldier's stories of their experiences?" She shook her head. She had, but not since high school. "They always talk about a bond of brotherhood that unites them, a bond forged in combat. It's because those men had to suffer their mortality together, to see just how fragile their lives were. Like when a mine blows up the guy next to you instead of you. Or when a shell explodes and turns the guy next to you into pieces but leaves you unharmed. When a bullet misses you and hits your buddy. Those men that survive are united in their sufferings, because of what they experienced.

"I'm not going to say that JP and I have that sort of brotherhood. But we do have a common struggle and in it we find strength with each other."

Bridget understood now what Sly meant. The strongest of bonds were forged in the hottest of crucibles.

By this point they were approaching Bridget's apartment, and she realized she would ordinarily be waking up now.

"Oh no," she said aloud. "I just realized I'm supposed to work today."

"Oh, yeah," Sly mumbled, almost forgetful that other people had to work.

"I guess I can just call in sick. Tammy will probably be pissed, but whatever."

Sly said nothing, but Bridget got the impression that he was suddenly regretful.

They got to the intersection right in front of her place, which did not have a traffic light, so they would have to dodge the morning rush hour.

"Can we just walk to the light?" Sly asked, pointing two blocks down the street.

"That'll take too long. I'm freezing," Bridget said. Truth be told, while she was very cold, her feet were growing extremely sore from wearing heels for almost fourteen hours, and she hadn't been able to properly feel her legs since they left the bar. "Let's just cross here."

"We're gonna have to run, though," Sly said.

"Okay. I'm going to grab your hand so I don't slip, and so you don't disappear," she said, releasing his arm and taking his hand. He seemed apprehensive to grip any harder than a light grasp. "I'll watch to the right, you watch to the left and tell me if we can make it across."

"Okay," Sly said, turning to his left and watching traffic.

"We're good here," she said.

"Not here," Sly answered. She turned and watched a car moving slowly enough that they could've crossed. A couple cars went by.

"Good here," she said again.

"Nope," Sly said. A few more cars went by.

"We're clear," she said, this time turning to look Sly's direction before he could answer.

"Car," he said. While a car was coming, Bridget knew if they hustled they could make it across the intersection.

"Let's go!" she cried as she jumped into the street, dragging Sly with her.

"Foxy!" he shouted as he allowed himself to get yanked into traffic.

The two rushed precariously into oncoming traffic and realized there was a rather sizable snow bank on the other side of the street. They didn't have time to go around it at this point.

"Jump!" she shouted as they got to the snow bank.

"Foxy!" Sly shouted again. He was able to crest the snow bank in a single step, but she was not so lucky, getting a bit stuck in the snow, which Sly managed to help pull her out of.

"That was crazy," she said breathlessly.

Suddenly, she heard the most terrifying voice in the world behind her. "Bridget?"

"That was crazy," Sly agreed as he brushed snow off his leg, totally oblivious to someone calling for Bridget. Bridget let go of his hand swiftly and turned to face the person who had said her name.

"Bridget," Ryan said again, this time not as a question.

"Uh, hey, Ryan," she said, frozen on the spot.

"Bridget?" Sly asked, looking at her, one eyebrow raised.

"What's going on here?" Ryan asked, studying each of them in turn.

"I, uh, I," she stammered. She was completely speechless, rooted to the spot. She had not foreseen this. What could she say?

"What's going on here?" Ryan reiterated, fury rising from his tone.

"I-I- it's not what it looks like," Bridget said, panic taking hold of her as she looked from Sly to Ryan.

"What is it?" Ryan asked.

In her absolute desperation she found herself repeating the same thing, "It's not what it looks like."

"Well then you better answer," Ryan fumed, "because I know what it looks like." By now he was staring furiously at Bridget.

"I-I-I." She stammered and stuttered but no words were coming to her as she stared at Ryan, trying to tell him with her eyes that it was not what he thought it was. "I-I. Sly-Sly tell him."

She turned to Sly, but he was gone!

"Where is he?" Ryan almost shouted, turning and realizing that he had disappeared. "Where'd he go?" Ryan started looking all over.

Bridget whipped her head in all directions; there was no sign of him. Sly had blinked into the next night.

"What the hell is going on?" he raged, taking a step toward her.

"I'm sorry, I'm sorry," she continued to be unable to say more than one thing on repeat. "I can't do this right now, I'm too tired, I'm too, too. . ." but she couldn't finish her sentence she was so overwhelmed. Between the long night, the hunger, and the emotional roller coaster of last night, everything had suddenly crescendoed and shattered right here. She was hopelessly overwhelmed.

"I have to go to work. We're still on mandatory overtime," Ryan explained through gritted teeth. "But you better be able to explain this to me when I get home tonight. And you better be home."

"I will, I will," she cried. With that Ryan stormed off to his car without another word. Bridget stood there, hot tears running down her face before finally running into her apartment building.

# CHAPTER 13

# The Aftermath

---

B ridget snapped out of her daze as she heard the front door to her apartment slam shut. She had been sleeping on and off throughout the day on the couch, sleep being her only escape from the mountain of emotion she seemed to be buried under. Even when she did doze, she was only able to sleep because she was utterly exhausted from the previous night's gallivanting. While she had made breakfast, she had eaten next to nothing since then. She had wondered last night why Ryan had never called or texted her, but earlier that day she had found her phone plugged into the speakers in their apartment; she had forgotten to take it to the bars. She had been trying to figure out what to tell Ryan throughout the day, but her brain seemed not to want to help her.

Time was up, however, and Ryan was home now—the door slamming shut was his herald.

"Hey," she said as she saw him enter the room. He said nothing in reply as he went to the sink. She looked out the window and saw that it was dark outside still.

"What time is it?" she asked.

"9:30," he said tersely, filling a glass with water.

"Oh, wow. I slept the whole day away," she said mostly to herself. "How was work?"

"Listen," Ryan said, leaning heavily on the counter. Bridget could see bags under his eyes, and his face was sweaty and a little dirty. "I don't know what that was this morning, but you had better explain yourself right now. I'm still on mandatory overtime, so this is the only chance you're going to get. What was that?"

Bridget knew it was time to own up. She couldn't lie to him. Despite what this morning had looked like, she was still in love with Ryan, and lying would be all it would take to undo what they had worked so hard for, especially these last couple months.

"That was my friend, Sly," she started. "I met him through a friend one night. He was just taking me home this morning. He just grabbed my hand because—well, no, I grabbed his hand so that I wouldn't slip."

"Why was *he* taking you home? And why did you need to be taken home? Where were you all night?" Ryan asked through clenched teeth.

"Because we were up all night at the bars," she explained shortly.

"The bars aren't open past 2am," he replied pointedly.

"Sly knew one of the bartenders on Brady Street really well, so he kept the bar open just for us."

Ryan was clearly suspicious, and while she was not being totally forthright with him, she was not telling him anything untrue.

"Where did he disappear to?" Ryan asked, clearly just as perturbed by that fact as seeing him holding Bridget's hand.

"I," she started. Now came the moment of truth. She could try to explain Sly's story, but would Ryan believe that? If Ryan didn't buy this part, he wouldn't believe anything else she had said. Now she understood why Sly and JP never talked about it with others. Who could possibly believe a story like that out of the blue? There was no way Ryan would believe her, and what was the point of telling the truth if no one would believe it?

She realized she needed to answer right there. "I don't know. I think he got a little scared because he knew that I had a boyfriend and you were probably him."

"But he didn't run off," Ryan tried to reason. "I would've seen or heard him if he did."

"Did you keep your eye on him the whole time?"

"No," Ryan scoffed. "But I still would've noticed him if he tried to run or leave."

"I don't know," Bridget said cryptically.

Ryan took a deep sigh, still leaning on the counter.

"Next time, you cannot forget your phone," he scolded her.

"Okay," she replied sheepishly.

His two long work days—plus staring at another twelve-plus hour day—had clearly sapped Ryan of his energy and emotion. Ryan grabbed a glass off the counter, refilled it with water and took a long drink, emptying the glass. Then he leaned over the counter and bowed his head as he exhaled long and slow.

Bridget had no idea what he was going to say. Was he going to demand more information, tell her he didn't believe her, tell her he didn't trust her anymore? She waited in anxious fear.

Finally, he raised his head and said simply, "If that's what you say happened. . . I believe you." Bridget felt a big release in her stomach. He stood up straight and started taking his work shirt off. "I'm going to bed," he said simply as he started towards the bedroom.

"Wait," Bridget said meekly.

"Good night," he replied decisively. He closed the door to the bedroom behind him.

Bridget sat there, uncertain if she should join him in the same bed tonight or remain on the couch.

# CHAPTER 14

# Conflicting Engagements

---

A month later, Bridget found herself at work getting scolded by Tammy for the umpteenth time.

"Also," Tammy said to Bridget. "Do you remember what I told you about work appropriate apparel?"

"No!" Bridget shot back, fully aware of the conversation Tammy had with Bridget about two weeks ago.

"Then you need to remember because the next time you wear something this. . . risqué, I'm going to have to do something about it," Tammy said as she walked away from Bridget and back to her office.

Bridget had had enough. This job was the worst, officially. Totally the worst. Liz had been promoted to another firm in Des Moines or someplace in Flatland, America, and had taken the job; she admitted to Bridget that even though she loved Milwaukee, Tammy was the reason she was leaving. Much to Bridget's frustration, Marissa had quit her job in anticipation of getting married, and another one of Bridget's work friends had taken another job because of Tammy. Of all her friends, Bridget had played the fool in this, opting to stay and hope for the best. Deep down, she had thought that if enough people quit or transferred, Tammy would get fired. Yet, after the highest turnover rate in company history, Tammy was still here.

The issue in question today was Bridget's choice of apparel for work, the same as it had been two weeks ago, the same as it had been almost a month ago. Spring had sprung early in Milwaukee, and Bridget had responded by daring to bare her legs at work. She had worn something similar the last couple days, but only today had it become a problem. Bridget was more than willing to bet Tammy was so on edge because the fiscal year was over and reports were coming in, and they were telling the same story that the employee turnover rate was.

Tammy's office door closed, and Bridget stared at her empty coffee mug seething with frustration. Then she looked at the time: 2:13. She dejectedly realized there was no way she was going to make it to the end of the day like this. Standing up and grabbing her things, she walked emotionally to Tammy's secretary and said, "I have to meet an old client at 2:30, I won't be back in the office today."

"I see," said the secretary, trying to sound suspicious, but nodding and signaling with her eyes that she understood Bridget's real reason for leaving.

With that, Bridget rushed home.

Bridget sat at home and binged her favorite TV show the rest of the afternoon until she heard the door open and close and knew Ryan was home. Jumping off the couch, she rushed to greet him, sliding in her socks as she did.

"Babe!" she said as she rushed into his arms.

"Bridg, babe, what's up?" he asked. Bridget rarely jumped to greet him at the door so something had to be up.

"I had the worst day of work EVER," she stated emphatically.

"What happened?" Ryan asked, concern on his face.

She recounted Tammy's passive-aggressiveness that day, as well as her sins from the last couple months in charge, going into detail how she especially felt victimized.

She finished with a sigh. Ryan was still standing there with his work things in hand, Bridget realized, so she let him pass.

As he did, he remarked, "Well, it sounds like you wanna quit."

"Oh my gosh, yes," the words were out before she could stop herself. She immediately regretted her forwardness, even if it was how she actually felt.

"I mean, if you really hate it that much, I think you should leave," Ryan said simply. He seemed to be taking this news too well.

"You really think so?" she asked.

"Yeah. I mean, what's the point in working a job that you hate?" he asked simply.

"I guess," Bridget said. She had been bracing for him to say that she should stick it out a bit longer and then decide. The two moved into the kitchen, where Ryan set about looking for a snack while Bridget sat on the stool by the counter.

"What will you do if you quit, though? Ryan asked.

Bridget wanted to say she wasn't sure, but again, before she could stop herself, she answered, "I think I want to be a teacher."

"A teacher?" Ryan asked, his eyebrows rising in surprise. "What makes you say that?"

"I think," she started, but paused herself. She had never talked about this with him before, only Sly. Was she really ready to tell him about this? She had to, she decided. "I think, I always wanted to be a teacher. But I was always scared away by their salaries."

Ryan nodded. "Yeah, I hear that."

"What do you think?" she asked him.

He shrugged. "Do you really want to do it, be a teacher? That's not the easiest job. I have a few buddies from high school that are teachers now. It's a tough job. You have to really love it."

"Oh, yeah, sure," Bridget replied, chewing on Ryan's advice.

Ryan continued, "I've never heard you say something about it before. Are you sure about this?"

"I don't know," Bridget replied sheepishly.

"You'd have to go back to school to get your license, right? That's a big commitment for something you don't know if you'd like." Ryan was doing a great job discouraging her to be a teacher right now.

"I think I've always wanted to do it, though," she reiterated.

"Okay," Ryan answered through a mouthful of cheese and crackers. "You remember my sister's husband, Jaime? He's a teacher now." Bridget nodded. "I know before he got a full-time position he spent a year subbing with a sub agency. You could try that. It's not great pay, but it's something. Then you can try it out before you commit to something you may not actually want to do."

"Hmm," she thought. Ryan might be onto something with this. The prospect of not making much money suddenly felt more real to her, and she mentally recoiled a bit. However, she absolutely could not stay at her current job. She hated it, absolutely hated it. And at this point, even Tammy leaving may not be enough to save it for her.

On the other hand, it was mid-March. She wouldn't have to work it too long before she could decide if it was what she wanted to do. Maybe this was worth a shot after all.

"What do I have to do?"

"Not too much, I think," Ryan said, trying to recall the process. "I think you just have to apply to an agency, tell them you need a license and want to work for them. They'll help you the rest of the way."

"Yeah," Bridget nodded. She suddenly thought about surrendering her current salary for a sum of maybe $100 a day, no benefits, no PTO if she was a sub. Not easy living. How would she cover all her expenses? She had the thought that she could make it work if it was really worth it. Either that, she reasoned, or returning to work beneath Tammy's thumb. "I-I think I want to try that."

"Okay," Ryan said. "I'll call my sister later and see what she can tell me about it, okay?" Bridget nodded, a small smile creeping onto her face.

\*     \*     \*     \*     \*

March came and went, and spring arrived as April did. Bridget applied to a sub agency, and, just as advertised, they helped her the rest of the way to getting certified, a process of only a few weeks. Then she took a week of paid time off at her job and taught for a week. She loved it immediately. She submitted her two weeks' notice right after and was more than happy to empty her desk and turn over all her accounts. For two weeks she was so happy telling Tammy off whenever she approached her. Bridget was almost sad to leave by the end.

By late April she had taught in four different school districts in the Milwaukee area, and had subbed for everything from second-grade to high school honors. While she was just a sub, she could see how much fun the job could be for her. Even just as a substitute teacher, when she was actually given something to teach, it gave her a feeling of satisfaction that her old job did only on its best days. After a couple weeks, she realized being with kids—the type of people that need the most help and guidance—and actually helping them grow was one of the most satisfying things. Even at the rougher schools, if she could just get through to one kid, it was a good day.

It was at this time that Ryan proposed to take her out for a very nice dinner. As he put it, he wanted to make it up to her for how dismal their three-year anniversary had been. Bridget thought it an unusual request from Ryan. Given that she had yet to wear the dress she had bought specifically for that dinner, she happily agreed.

"Oh, wow," Bridget said as they took their seat in the poshest restaurant in town. "This place is so nice."

"Yep," Ryan said. "That's why we're here."

"Thank you," she said with a big smile, reaching across the table to hold his hand.

The night was going so well. They were laughing, sharing old stories, talking about the future, it was all so wonderful. The spark was back, she felt. When Ryan went to the restroom, she had a moment to reflect. For the first time in years, she felt something from Ryan, a giddiness, a nervousness almost; he just seemed so happy to be with her again. He was acting like they were on their first date again. Oh, that first date was wonderful; he had shown flashes of suave brilliance mixed with the sheepishness and silliness that comes with a first date.

Ryan returned from the bathroom and sat down, reaching across the table to hold both her hands, which she happily allowed.

"Bridget," he started, "I'm so happy I have you in my life." He smiled at her.

"Me, too," she said.

"And I'm really thankful that you took the initiative to sit down and have that discussion back around Christmas. It's made a world of difference."

"Aw, thank you," Bridget answered bashfully. She had felt so much better about them ever since that talk, too. And tonight seemed to be the culmination of all the hard work and good feelings it had engendered.

"I know our third anniversary wasn't quite what either of us wanted it to be," he started, as champagne arrived, seemingly unasked for by Ryan or Bridget. "But I'm hoping we'll have many more."

"What's this for?" Bridget asked, confused by the arrival of champagne.

"Well, tonight is a special occasion," Ryan said, releasing her hands.

"But it's not actually our anniver–" she started. Then she bolted upright in her chair as it suddenly hit her what was going on. Ryan reached into his pocket and pushed his chair back, standing up.

"No, it's better," he answered her half-asked question. He walked around the table right up to her and dropped to one knee with a big smile on his face. "It's the night we get engaged."

She threw her hands to her mouth in complete shock.

"Bridget Mary Young," he said, holding forth a felt ring box and opening it to reveal a ring that dazzled in the many lights of the restaurant. "Will you marry me?"

She was in shock. A wave of emotion rushed over her, and everything around her seemed to stop. She tried to move her hands, but they seemed frozen in place, covering her open mouth. She finally managed to put her hands down and stared in stark wonder at the spectacular jewel before her.

Finally, she found the strength to answer. After what felt like an eternity, she responded, "Yes."

# CHAPTER 15

# Confessions

---

Bridget and Ryan were getting married. She was so excited. They hadn't done any detailing about when or where, but they were getting married. Bridget had been blown away by just how much work Ryan had put into the proposal, especially because it was his first great initiative in their relationship in a long time. She and Ryan had spent the next week madly in love with each other, staring into each other's eyes, touching foreheads, whispering nicknames to each other, and all manner of other things. Bridget even went through the trouble of dressing up super nice for him one night, even though they were only staying in. She made sure to wear her leather skirt for him. The feeling of new love was something she had been missing for so long.

Her emotional high subsided after that week, but the excitement was still there. She had decided that this was actually what their relationship had needed, something new and fresh, something to talk about and be excited for. Through all of April she felt this way, but then even that excitement started to wane. Bridget realized that after that night, nothing about them had changed. They were still doing all the same things they had been for the weeks and months prior. Ryan seemed even more invested in work lately, and by the time May came, he seemed to be over the feeling of getting married, too. They were engaged, but beside that, nothing about them was different.

As that first week in May reached Thursday, Bridget noticed that she had this nagging feeling that would not go away: Sly. She was incredibly torn about him emotionally, and she had an unsavory feeling about their last, forced parting. She would catch herself day-dreaming about them gallivanting through the morning, showing him all the things he couldn't do at night. When she would catch herself, she would spiral into her old regret loop: regret for daydreaming about Sly, but not thinking it a big deal, then regretting that she felt that way. Finally she decided she couldn't live like this, she couldn't live with herself being engaged to one man but always thinking about another.

She knew Ryan would be working late taking a conference call from Taiwan, so this was as good a chance as she would get. She decided it was time to go back to Mike's on Brady. She *needed* to go back to Mike's on Brady.

The traffic seemed to help her, as she got there in record time without really trying to. She almost wished it had taken longer so she would've had more time to think. As she parked her car, she had the thought that she couldn't do this, she shouldn't. She closed her eyes, put both hands on her head, and took a deep breath. Regardless of whether she should or shouldn't, she had to do this.

She got out, walked down the street, and walked into Mike's. It was an easy task to find Sly, he was in the same spot as usual. She was shocked, however, to realize that as she saw him, she immediately remembered their last meeting. Not how it had ended, but how much fun it had been, more fun than she'd had in years, in fact. . . She shook the thought and approached him.

"Hey, Sly," she said, feeling very small as she did.

"Oh," Sly said, in slightly exaggerated surprise. "Hey, *Bridget*. If that's your real name."

"I'm sorry," she said. "I shouldn't have lied to you like that. I thought you were making up your name, so, I just-I just made up my own name."

Sly sat in irate silence.

"I'm sorry," Bridget apologized. A long silence settled between them. This was not how Bridget had expected it to go. An argument would be better than this. "I don't know what else to say. I don't know what else you want me to say."

Sly seemed to be battling with the idea of tearing into her and just riding this out. He exhaled slowly, bowing his head as he did, and then simply said, "I understand."

"Thanks," she said after a pause. "I quit my job," she followed up suddenly, "because of the stuff you told me. The stuff we talked about."

For the first time that night, Sly seemed to cool off a bit. He turned to face her. "Really?" On his face, Bridget could tell that his anger had abated, but he was still at least annoyed. However, she also read that he was genuinely—maybe even pleasantly—surprised by her reveal.

"Yes," she said, "about a month ago. I work as a substitute teacher now."

"Really?" Sly asked. He paused as he digested that bit of news. "I didn't think you ever would. Good for you."

"Thanks," she said slowly, peeved that he had doubted her.

"So then you are going to pursue your dream of being a teacher?" he asked.

She nodded and answered, "Yes. I love it, actually. It's everything I had hoped it could be. I'm going to take night classes and get certified for full-time work."

"That's great," Sly said, the impact of this surprise clearly having broken a lot of the cold feelings between them.

"Also," she started, far more apprehensively this time. "Ryan and I, uh, we, uh, we patched things up after he. . . met you, I guess."

"I can tell," Sly said without looking at her, only holding up his hand and wiggling his ring finger. "It's very nice."

"Thanks," she said again.

Now Sly turned fully to face her, and looked her right in the eye as he asked, "I thought you didn't want to get married?"

Of all the things she wasn't sure about tonight, she knew he would ask her this. He was right, she had said that to him, and a couple times at that. Yet, here she was after all the problems she had come to him for—the problems in her and Ryan's relationship—with a ring on her finger.

"I know I said that," she answered. "I don't know. I guess it was one of those things I didn't know I wanted it until I got it." Her voice seemed to falter before she had finished. She knew Sly didn't buy that.

Sly chuckled, then put his palm on the bar counter. He took a deep breath and closed his eyes, then bowed his head and nodded; perhaps only to himself, Bridget thought.

"Do you love him?" Sly asked, not looking up or opening his eyes.

Bridget was unprepared for that question.

"Do you really love him? More than life itself?"

She had braced for him to tell her everything she had done wrong again, but his question seemed simple enough. "Yes," she answered, steeling herself. In that moment, though, she realized the real reason she had come to Mike's tonight, the real reason she wanted to see Sly. While her brain had told her not to come, her heart had told her she needed to.

"Yes," she said again, "I do really love him."

"More than life itself?" Sly asked again, unconvinced, quickly turning to her.

"Yes," she said, now clearly struggling for words. "I do love him, but. . ." Sly sat up and started chewing the inside of his lip as Bridget finished, "not as much as someone else."

Sly closed his eyes and sighed with a look of exhaustion on his face. "Who is it?" he asked, but Bridget knew that he already had the answer.

"You," she said, in her quietest voice possible. She started to shake a little bit after she said it; even she didn't feel ready for that revelation. Why did she say that? Did she mean it? Why would she have said it if she didn't mean it?

"No," he said at last.

"What?" Bridget asked, both hurt and surprised. His one word seemed to cut her like an icy knife.

"No, you don't," Sly said, his frustration clearly beginning to overwhelm him.

"I do," she tried to defend herself, but she knew that she was trying to build a wall of paper against the storm that Sly would come at her with.

"What have you ever done for me?" he asked, suddenly standing up. She felt as if he were about to attack her. "What have you ever gone out of your way to do for me? When have you ever asked about my life, or my hopes, or my dreams—before or with my condition? When have you ever done something for me with my well-being or my interests being the main and only reason?"

He paused tersely. "What have you ever sacrificed for me?"

He suddenly seemed ferocious; she had not seen anything like this from him at any point before now. She began to feel some fear and anguish as he began to verbally flog her.

"This thing here—this thing between us—whatever it is, it is not love. It's nothing like love. And I never claimed it was, but you clearly have.

In fact, I don't think you understand love at all. You claimed you never wanted to get married, and now you're newly engaged, but then you're telling someone else that you love them, someone you *barely* know. You don't understand what love is.

"Love, in the simplest sense, is the entire giving of yourself to another person, to someone else, and then that person doing the same for you. That's what love is and that's what it takes. It's a two-way street. I may never have experienced love, it's painfully obvious to me that you haven't either."

Bridget felt as if she had just been ripped to pieces, shredded by his cutting words. She could not help the tears welling in her eyes now.

"Would you," Sly asked, much slower and more controlled than before, "if you could—if by some mystical twist of fate—take my condition, my burden, at the expense of everything you've ever wanted: a home, a purpose, and love? Would you be willing to give everything you have for me? That's the cost of love."

Tears were flowing down her face now. She didn't know if anyone else was in the bar, but she didn't care now. All she could feel right now was the merciless words of this man before her.

"I would!" she cried to him, "I would!"

Sly answered, surprising calmly, "No you wouldn't," before sitting back on his stool. Then he said the words that would send her from the bar back into the night, broken.

"Your words, like your love, are empty."

Her composure shattered with his final stab; she was defeated, broken, cast down. She felt rooted to the spot, she felt as if she could not see or hear anything, only feel the wound of his parting words. Without any other recourse, she ran from Sly, crying uncontrollably as she did.

She threw the door open back into a cold, early spring rain that had begun to pour. Over the sound of the rain, she never heard Sly mutter, "I never want to see you again."

She ran, heedless of the downpour around her, running with one purpose: to get away from Mike's on Brady. She rushed to her car and threw herself inside as she continued to weep ceaselessly.

She wept and wept until she had nearly cried herself to exhaustion. The she realized she couldn't go home like this; she was a total wreck, and then Ryan would wonder what had happened and she would have to explain herself. She couldn't face that, not now, maybe not ever. What was she to do? She couldn't tell Ryan, she couldn't bear to tell her mother or her friends or anyone. For the first time, Sly had been the one to cut her down rather than raise her up.

In that moment, she experienced a fleeting sensation of what it meant to live like Sly: she had nothing, nowhere to go home to.

# CHAPTER 16

# Voices in the Night

———

Back in the bar Sly drained the rest of his drink and promptly asked for another one. JP walked over to him.

"You, good?" he asked Sly.

"Fine," Sly muttered.

JP poured him another tap. "That was quite a scene, dude."

"It had to be done," Sly replied frankly, taking his beer and gulping down almost half of it. JP waited patiently for Sly to continue.

"I'm not talking about what you said, I'm talking about how you said it," JP clarified.

"She needed to hear it," Sly said. "I do like her, more than I'd like to admit. But I do not love her, and I will never love her." He took another swig.

"Why," JP asked, taking Sly head on.

"She's completely blind to reality," Sly stated bluntly. "If she thinks she knows love, then she doesn't know anything. Maybe her and her fiancé have love, but if so, it is entirely by accident." Sly was looking around more than usual in his agitation.

JP asked, "How can you know whether or not they have it if you've never experienced it?"

"Because I don't need to," Sly said straightforward. "Because I sit here and watch the people that come to these bars and frequent the streets at night, the types of people that pass the word 'love' around as you or I might pass this glass about in a night. I see what they do, what they define as love." He took a long drink.

"None of it is. The one thing about love that I know is this: If you love until it hurts, there can be no more hurt, only love."

JP nodded in small awe. "That's beautiful."

"The reason I know that I have never encountered love," Sly began, "is because all I encounter is hurt. Hurt people. That's all I see in these bars, and that's all that really exists for people like us: hurt. If loving 'til it hurt meant that there could be no hurt, then I know that I've never encountered love. At this point I don't even know if love can really exist in this cruel world."

JP nodded his head over and over as he churned through the words in his mind.

"What is love, then?" JP asked at last.

Sly leaned heavily on the bar, his labors seeming to have sapped his strength. Nodding and staring at the bar top, he said in reply, "What do you think love is?"

JP thought intensely in the silence. As he did, his demeanor seemed to lighten a bit. "A spark," he said at last. "A spark that can be found in all kinds of places. A passing glance, a thoughtful gaze, an open ear, a kiss. Love is any moment when one soul finds a moment of embrace in another's. That's what I believe love is."

JP continued, inspired, waxing poetry, "The great burden of love, so to speak, is turning that one small spark, the tiniest of sparks, into a roaring fire that can burn all through the ages of humanity, a fire that can blaze through whatever lies in the path of those who share it: tragedy, sorrow, heartbreak, fear, despair, hatred. A light that can scatter the darkness before it and banish the night.

"It needs constant care and attention, though. Failure to feed the fire for a time is not death to love, because a fire can burn long after it ceases to be fed fuel. But going too long without feeding it will lead to an inevitable and permanent burnout. When the fire is finally reduced to smoldering remains and then to ashes, it cannot be relit. Love is the same."

JP finished his musings and nodded to himself, almost as if to admit that was the first time he had ever put his thoughts to words.

"I'm impressed," Sly said with a smile. "That was poetry, JP, poetry." JP nodded to himself, believing he had defined this great enigma. "You gave the best description of love I've ever heard, but you haven't really defined it."

"I assume you've got something then?" JP asked.

"Love," Sly began, "means caring for someone else more than you care for yourself. It means putting the person you love ahead of you in every way. Their dreams, their hopes, their needs, their wants. Love is a measure of how much you're willing to give for that other person. The more willing you are to give for them, the more you love them. The greatest form of love is to give up your life itself. Not always *actually* giving it up, but being *willing* to give it up."

Sly paused for a drink.

"I know that Bridget doesn't love me because I know that if there was really some way for her to take my curse and take my place in the night so that I could be free and whole again, she wouldn't take it. She says she would, but she'd waffle, and hesitate, and think about it, and then she would sheepishly say no. Or," he put his finger up, "on the off chance she would take it willingly, she would only take it because she does not understand the weight of the burden we carry. In time, the crushing weight of it would break her and fill her with regret. In the end she would not have love, only hurt.

"That's why I say that I will know love when I find it. If I ever found someone willing—entirely *willing*—to take my suffering from me at the cost of their whole life, that would be love."

JP exhaled, satisfied by Sly's reply. "I see. That's a tall order."

"It is," Sly acknowledged, "but so is love. I think deep down everyone knows exactly how tall an order it is, and they are terrified to death of it. So they bastardize it, diminish it. People have dragged the name of love into the dirt so they can possess it without sacrifice. I even explained this to Bridget, but—like I said—she's too blind to see this.

"That's also how I know that Bridget and her fiancé do not have love."

JP nodded, having taken in everything Sly had proclaimed and still wanting more. "So, is her fiancé a bad guy? Or Bridget a bad girl?"

Sly shook his head. "No, I don't think either of them are bad people, per say. But I do think they've lost their way. See, to me, love isn't about finding *anyone*, it's about finding *someone*. It's about waiting for that person who, like you said, finds their soul's embrace in another."

"What makes a person a *someone*?" JP asked, stroking his beard thoughtfully.

Sly looked up at JP, measuring his response. "Not being afraid of being alone."

JP seemed surprised by that answer. "How do you figure?"

"It's not that complicated," Sly began, waving his hand. "Someone like Bridget is always running for friends, or her fiancé, or me, or whomever. She wants to feel safe and insulated. The last thing she wants to be is alone, by herself. The reason is simple: in those moments, she doesn't have anything to distract her from the fact that she gave up on her dreams."

"Ah," JP breathed.

Sly continued. "People hate being alone because when they are, they have to confront the fact that they aren't being the person they really want to be. They know it deep down all the time, but they try to drown it out by any means necessary. Most often, they do it by trying to find a relationship, because then they have proof that at least one other person doesn't see them the way they see themselves. The problem is that is a toxic relationship from before it even begins, and any love found in it is purely accidental.

"That's how you can know a *someone* when you find them. They not only live with themselves, they are happy with who they are. They don't need any validation from anyone else about who they are. They have to love themselves—not in a narcissistic way, but in a sincere, honest way. If you can't love yourself, how can you love someone else?"

Sly took another drink while JP nodded silently to himself.

"No, Bridget and Ryan are not bad people, they are just bad for each other. They are holding each other back from being *someone*."

"Hm," JP grunted. A short pause lingered between them, and then—to Sly's supreme surprise—JP laughed. "How have we never talked about his before?"

"Because nothing we talk about will change anything," Sly replied pessimistically. "We're just voices in the night."

# CHAPTER 17

# The Empty Bed

---

The last two days had been awful for Bridget. She had declined to take a sub job that next day after her conversation with Sly, instead spending the majority of the time Ryan was at work crying. For how upset and confused she was by everything, it was all made worse by the fact that she couldn't tell Ryan any of this; anything she told him would demand more questions and answers she was not ready to give. Now, most of Saturday she had been very quiet and soberly thoughtful, barely leaving her bed.

Sly's words had echoed in her head endlessly, incessantly. That she didn't love him; that she didn't know love; that her words, like her love, were empty. The one that stung most, however, was his question of would she take his burden from him, followed by his accusation that no, she wouldn't. That one hurt most of all, she realized, because it was true. As much as she hated that fact, as much as she wanted to deny it, it was true. She wouldn't trade her life, her freedom for his burden. Her freedom and his burden. Over the past two days she had come to understand that for how much her freedom and independence were her identity, his burden was his identity. Somehow, to her, they seemed intertwined. In his state, he had no freedom, but for her, she seemed lost in her identity despite her freedom.

"Honey," she said at last, calling to Ryan in the kitchen from her post on their bed; she was sitting there cross-legged and had not moved in about an hour.

"Yeah, what's up, Bridg?" he asked, staying in the kitchen. Ryan had asked her several times what was wrong, but she just said she was wasn't feeling well.

"Babe," she said again, after he didn't come into the room.

"Yeah, what's up?" he asked again, finally having arrived. "You doing okay?"

She nodded shortly. "I just don't feel too well."

"You want me to make something? Soup or tea or anything?"

She shook her head.

"What's up?"

"What would you do for me?" she asked.

Ryan looked at her, utterly baffled by the question, making a confused face as he did. "What?"

"What would you do for me?" she asked.

He stood in the doorway pondering. "Anything," he said at last, walking over to the bed to sit by her. "That's why we're getting married, because I'd do anything for you." He leaned in and kissed her, and she lifelessly returned it.

"What's up?" Ryan asked again, sensing she was off.

"Would you stay with me," she started, "if you could never live in the day again? If every time the sun came up you would disappear until nightfall?"

"I'm sorry," Ryan said, clearly confused again. "What?"

"Would you stay with me if you could never live in the daytime again? No job, no career, no friends, no summer days, no sunshine, no sunrise. Would you stay with me if you couldn't have those?" she asked.

Ryan stared at her, confused and thoughtful. "Yeah," he said at last. "Yeah, sure. I mean, that would never happen, but . . . yeah, I'd stay."

She said nothing in response, only bit both her lips as her jaw trembled.

"You okay?" Ryan asked, leaning away from her.

She nodded. They sat in uncomfortable silence.

"What about you?" he asked. "Would you stay with me if you could only—only live in the night or whatever?"

It took all of her willpower to hold her composure as she felt tears press against her eyes. She started nodding weakly before, almost in a whisper, she answered, "Yes."

Ryan nodded his head, unsure of what exactly was going on.

"I'm fine," she said at last, regaining control over her thoughts just long enough to form a coherent sentence. "I just need some time."

"Okay," Ryan said, nodding but not standing up. After a few moments, he finally stood up and walked toward the door.

"Close the door please," she said quickly.

He turned to her in concern as he grasped the door handle. After a short pause, he walked out, pulling to door closed behind him.

*　*　*　*　*

"That was a lot of fun," Ryan said as he unbolted the door to their apartment and led Bridget inside, wiping his brow as he did. Even though it was early-June, the dog days of summer were upon them, and Milwaukee was cooking. They had just gotten back from a new hipster restaurant on Brewers Hill, which they went to for dinner. It was early evening and the sun was just starting to set, painting a beautiful canvas across the sky as it did.

"Yeah," she said simply.

"What did you think of the food?" Ryan asked.

"It was . . . it was decent. I'm not the biggest tomato person, but . . ." she answered.

"What's up?" Ryan asked, for what felt like the thousandth time in the past few months.

Bridget had spent the past few months torn between many things. It had been a very somber past few months, and while she seemed trapped inescapably in her own thoughts, Ryan seemed to be on the up-and-up with their relationship. He had started using nicknames with her again, he had started taking more initiative in making plans, he had started to be everything and do everything she had wanted and hoped him to be. Yet, now that he was doing all of those things—those things that six months ago would've made her the happiest girl in the world—now it all seemed far too insignificant. It seemed too little, too late. Bridget could trace it all back to one night: the night Sly had sent her crying from Mike's on Brady.

Everything that she could remember that Sly had told her since they met almost ten months ago seemed to echo to the depths of her very being. All his idealistic talk of love and happiness had been steadily growing deeper and deeper roots in her. As a result, it was slowly overturning everything that she knew. It was tearing Bridget apart.

Ever since she had professed her love for Sly, which she realized was a lie—as he had said—she had slowly come to the understanding that everything Sly had said about her was right. Now every time she told Ryan that she loved him, she felt a little more of her old self die away.

"So, Bridg," Ryan said, clearly wanting to talk about something. "Babe, I, uh, ha, I wanted to talk about our wedding."

She froze. She was not ready for this. While she showed no outward sign of emotion at his statement, she merely responded with, "What do you mean?"

"Well," he started, standing near the table and rocking one of the chairs on two legs with his hand, "Honey, it's been over two months since we got engaged, and, uh, we haven't talked once about when or where or how or any of that."

"I know," she said, a sense of dread building in her.

"Well, I mean," he started, "shouldn't we start planning something? If only a date and maybe a venue?"

Bridget nodded, realizing that this was not going to be an easy night. "Yes."

"Good," Ryan said, measuring her mood. He pulled a chair out for her and beckoned her to sit, which she did so begrudgingly. Then he took a seat himself. "I was thinking," he started, still measuring her mood, "we could have a small ceremony, somewhere local. It'll save money and it'll still be great. Then we can put more money into the reception." She said nothing in the pause that followed. "So, if you're okay with that, then we just have to figure out a date." He paused again. "What are you thinking?"

Bridget needed some time to muster her response. "I think," she started heavily, "now's not the best time."

He sighed. "It's been two months. Some people get married two months after they get engaged. We haven't even talked about our wedding since. I thought you would be the one to bring it up and talk about it since you're the one who really wanted us to get married."

Bridget took a sharp halt in her thoughts. "Wait, what?" she asked.

"I was hoping that after this long you would've given me more to work with in regard to a venue and date and all of that stuff because I thought you were the one who really wanted to do this."

"Do what?" she asked, beginning to understand what was happening.

"Get married," Ryan said, growing impatient. "I proposed to you when I did because I thought you wanted to get married. I thought you were being impatient with me, but you never said anything, so I just had to work with what you gave me."

"You *only* proposed because you *thought* that's what I wanted?" She was floored at the notion.

"Well, that is what you want, right?" Ryan asked, clearly getting agitated.

"What do you want?" she found herself asking in a surprisingly Sly fashion.

"A straight answer," Ryan snapped.

Bridget snapped back, "Do you want to get married or did you do it just because you *think* I want to get married?"

"I want," Ryan took a deep breath, reaching over to her and grasping her hand, "whatever you want. I want to marry you. I want to start a life together. Soon." Bridget withdrew her hand. "Listen, Bridget, I know you told me way back when we started dating that you didn't want to get married. But then we had that date at the place right on the lake way back—oh I don't know when, it was close to Halloween, I think—and you kept giving me hints that you wanted to get married. You've been doing it a lot since then, too, what with wanting to go on more dates and spend more time just you and I together. You even got really jealous whenever I wanted to go out with the guys."

She started to fidget she was getting so frustrated. "No, Ryan," she proclaimed, "I didn't want to get married. I still don't want to get married. Why didn't you just ask me if that was what you were thinking?"

"Because," he started, finally losing his composure, "because I was afraid that you'd say you didn't want to get married but, deep down, you actually would want to."

"Then you should've trusted me," she said.

"Well," Ryan said, regaining his initiative, "I didn't buy that ring just so we could be engaged without actually planning to get married."

"I don't know if I want to get married right now!" Bridget shouted, finally beginning to meltdown.

"If you're not sure about that, then what's the point of being engaged?"

"It was so we could take the next step in our relationship!" she cried. "Because I'm still not sure if I want to marry you."

He balked at her. "You're not sure if you want to marry *me*?"

"No, not you," she said, her emotions starting to take over. "At all. I don't know if I want to get married *at all*."

"Well I'm not so certain I want to be with a woman who's almost thirty and doesn't know what she wants–"

"I'M TWENTY-EIGHT!" she shrieked at him. "Not almost thirty!"

"I can't do this right now," Ryan said, pushing his chair back and standing up. "I'm leaving for tonight. It may be time for us to reevaluate things." He walked to the door and slammed it shut on his way out.

As soon as the door slamming shut echoed through the hallway, Bridget broke into tears.

"What have I done?" she cried aloud, throwing her arms on the table and her face into her arms, weeping uncontrollably.

That evening she stayed up until well past midnight, tearfully waiting at the table for her fiancé to return to her. But he never came. It was almost 1:00AM when she finally retreated to her bedroom, clambering for the welcome embrace of her bed. But, for the first time in a long time, she had no one to hold her, only an empty bed.

# CHAPTER 18

# The Storm

———

B ridget woke up to the warm September morning sunshine; it was shining through the cheap Venetian blinds in her apartment. She had woken up, but wished she were still asleep. It was Sunday, and she was a little upset to have woken up so early. Sub teaching all the time meant she had to get up almost an hour earlier than when she had worked her old job. While teaching was absolutely worth it, being barely able to sleep past 7:30 on weekends was less than stellar. She rolled over in her bed and stretched out, covering the whole expanse of her simple twin bed.

She had been in her new place for just over a month-and-a-half, and she still wasn't too sure about how she felt about it. One thing she did know for sure, though: it was not her old place that she had with Ryan. Almost two months ago, the day after their fight over the fate of their relationship, Ryan had declared that they were done, and Bridget had not contested him. Then Ryan said he would stay at a buddy's place until she found somewhere to move if she gave him the ring back, which she did. It was a gesture, she thought, and a sign that while their love was over, there was no reason they couldn't be civil about a failed romance. Two weeks later she had moved into an old apartment building on Arlington just off Brady Street. It was small, old, somewhat rundown, and pretty cramped, but she had taken the place because it was cheap, clean, in a decent neighborhood, and did month-to-month leases.

Bridget had, unknowingly, come to the same conclusion that Sly had confided to JP: that while Bridget and Ryan were not bad or toxic people, they were just not in love. Everything between them was over. Ryan had allowed Bridget to take everything that they had purchased together, on the condition that she pay the fee for breaking their lease. All the loose ends had been tied off.

Bridget went through her Sunday much as she had the last few Sundays since she had become single again: alone. Sundays were the hardest for her. Those had been the days where she and Ryan would just relax and be together. Saturdays had always been cleaning day or grocery shopping day, or a day to get some other essential chores done. But Sundays, Sundays were the payoff, whether it was a movie, a long walk in the park, or going to visit each other's parents. While she still filled her Saturdays with cleaning and grocery shopping and such, Sundays were a gaping void to her now.

She had started going to church on Sunday mornings just to have something to do, there being one within walking distance on Brady Street. The afternoons, however, she dreaded. That was the time when she really had to grapple with just how alone she was. No one to watch TV or movies with, no one to walk in the park with.

She had worked very hard for Sundays not to be like this. A couple times she tried going to brunch with friends, but after two trips, her bank account told her she couldn't be spending that kind of money every Sunday. She had also tried to turn Sunday into beach days, but those were always hit or miss, and sometimes the weather conspired against her. She had gone to local bookstores and the library to read, but there were very few books she actually wanted to read; she loved reading romance, but now she wanted nothing to do with the genre. As summer came to a close and she realized beach days couldn't be a thing anymore, she tried to sleep Sunday away, but to no avail. Her tactic last night had been to get the girls together in the hope of staying out very late. While Steph had said she would love to, the other girls had said they were unavailable (Bridget had one bright spot in that Kim couldn't go because she was going to a movie with her own boyfriend). She started to wonder if Sundays would always be like this, and if there was anything else she could do to stop this feeling of loneliness and emptiness.

As Sunday morning stretched into Sunday afternoon, Bridget decided she needed to get out of the house. But where to go? And with whom? She wanted to leave her bed behind, but she decided to binge through some more of her favorite show for the umpteenth time before finally prying herself from the sheets just before a normal person's dinnertime.

She went for a long bike ride through the neighborhoods of the lower east side as the sun began its final approach to the horizon. She got home, showered, and made a simple dinner, chewing on her thoughts as much as she chewed on her food. The idea had come when she biked past the place, a place she had not been in months. The place where she had first realized that she and Ryan did not, despite her best efforts, love each other.

She finished her food and washed her dishes, trying to push the urge to go to Mike's out of her mind as she did. When she finished, she climbed back onto her bed and reached for her computer, but it did not turn on. It was dead. She would have to find the cord, which she was always losing in her tiny apartment. After a few frustrating minutes she gave up and realized that the only way to satisfy her urge to leave the apartment would be to actually leave the apartment.

As she left, she saw dark storm clouds gathering in the sky and heard the rumble of distant thunder; a late summer storm was rolling in. She had brought a raincoat, foreseeing such a turn in the weather. She walked the block to Brady Street and then a half block towards the lake, the first drops of rain falling as she pulled open the door to Mike's on Brady. As she stepped inside, she scanned the bar and was surprised that absolutely no one was there, not a single person other than JP tending the bar.

"Hello, Bridget," he said, glad that someone was patronizing the bar on a dreary Sunday afternoon.

"Hey, JP," she replied, looking around in confusion; where was Sly? She walked over the bar and sat down.

"What brings you in?" he asked.

"Uh," she started, looking around her.

"Ah," JP said, sticking his tongue into his lower lip. "I see. Well, I am disappointed to tell you this, but he isn't here today."

"What?" Bridget asked, shocked. "But he's always here."

"Not these days," JP said gravely.

"What happened?" Bridget exclaimed, suddenly fearful.

"He's just, he's not in Milwaukee anymore. A few weeks ago he said he couldn't take Milwaukee anymore. He had to go."

"Where did he go?" Bridget asked.

"Chicago. I think. He's gone there a few times since I've met him. That's where he goes when he feels Milwaukee is getting a little too small."

Bridget nodded her head knowingly. It was true, there were times when Milwaukee's little-big city feel could be as cramped as her new apartment. She sat there, unsure of what to do next when a loud boom sounded overhead, signaling the arrival of the late-summer storm.

"That was quick," JP remarked looking at the ceiling. The two remained in silence as sheets of rain started crashing upon the roof.

"Business always slows down when it rains," JP said. "And when it starts to get cold like it will tonight."

"What's his real name?" Bridget suddenly asked. "What's Sly's real name?"

"What do you mean?" JP asked, amused.

"Well, I've never heard you call him by his name, and I thought for sure he was making that name up. I mean, what parents name their kid 'Sly' unless they think he's going to be in a book or something?"

JP had a good chuckle to himself all through Bridget's question. "His name *is* Sly. His full name," he paused for effect, "is Sylvester."

"Oh, my gosh," Bridget said, disappointed in the fact that she had doubted Sly's honesty.

"I don't use his name because he's asked me not to. It's an unusual name, and I'm sure you can understand why he goes by Sly," JP said.

The two returned to silence, JP wiping down random glasses and the counter. As they remained in silence, Bridget began to blame Sly for losing everything she had a few short months ago. "I hate him."

"He has that effect on people," JP replied.

"I wish I had never met him." she said, defeated.

JP paused in his cleaning and glanced at her. "Because of everything you've lost?"

She nodded, her eyes getting warm.

"I understand the way you feel. There's one particular woman in my life I wish I hadn't met," JP replied cryptically. Bridget immediately forgot her own pain at JP's words.

"I'm so sorry for you," she replied.

He waved his hand. "Don't," he said shortly. "I'm this way for a reason."

Bridget gave pause. "What does that mean?"

JP gave her a look as if to ask how she didn't understand that. "What's happened to me has happened to me for a reason."

Bridget suddenly felt equally confused and sympathetic. "How can you say that?"

JP raised his eyebrows. "How can I say that? That's the only thing I can say. I don't have a life, I don't have dreams or ambitions, I don't have anything in my future. I have nothing to hold on—to keep me going—except the idea that maybe I'm this way for a reason."

Bridget stared at JP in small wonder. "How can you still feel that way after years like this?"

JP leaned over on the bar as he stared thoughtfully past her. Overhead, the thunder rolled on and the rains continued to batter the old bar. He sighed deeply.

"I've been a bartender long enough to know that nothing in this world happens by chance. I don't know how else to describe it other than the universe has this sort of intentionality to. It might be God, it might be something else. It's not a predestination thing, more of an understanding of the whole."

Bridget was staring at him like he had just told her the world was flat.

"Let me try an example, 'cause this gets hard to explain," he continued. "You know how in your favorite stories, no matter how rough things get throughout it, in the end, everything turns out alright? Life is the same way."

"So you think you have a fairy tale ending?" she interrupted, a little surprised that he would seem so cavalier about that notion.

"No," JP said simply. "I don't necessarily think that *I* have a fairy tale ending. I'm not the main character in the story of the universe. In books and movies, a lot of times, only the main character gets the fairy tale ending. Everyone else kind of stays the same, but they all have their part to play to get to the ending."

Bridget nodded skeptically.

"Most stories are only about twenty, thirty people, maybe," JP resumed, shaking his hand as he said maybe. "Some have more, some have less, but you get my point. There has never been a story about a million people, though, where we learn all their names and care about them all." He indicated to Bridget to see if she was following; she nodded, still skeptical, but warming up to it.

"My point is, the universe is a story, and every person who has ever lived has a role to play in it, and we are all just side characters. Some of us are good, some of us are bad. That also means that some of us get happy endings, some of us don't. Some of us have bigger roles to play than others. I don't know why some people get the roles and endings they do, but

I do believe it is for a reason. That's what I mean by intentionality of the universe, that it's writing our story."

Bridget nodded as she understood his point, but it didn't really make her feel better, and she didn't really buy it.

JP seemed to pick up on this, because he continued, with a mild smile. "You don't believe me. Alright, fair enough. So you're mad because you met Sly and everything fell apart. You think you could've done something to avoid this. Well, let me ask you something, how did you and Sly meet?

Bridget had to think back. "I-I went up to him one night, here."

JP shook his head, his smile getting bigger. "No. I remember it exactly. You didn't go up to him one night, this all started when *your friend* went up to him and tried to flirt with him. Something that *your friend* did with a stranger is what started you on this path."

Bridget suddenly recalled with outstanding clarity that first time she had ever set foot into Mike's on Brady and how she hadn't even noticed Sly until she saw Kim and Steph talking about him. Bridget suddenly had the realization that she would never have even noticed Sly if Kim hadn't first.

"Still think we write our own stories?" JP asked with a grin.

Bridget nodded in understanding. She was feeling very overwhelmed at this point between her lingering feeling of emptiness, her thoughts about all that JP had said, and her desperate desire not to go home and be alone.

Outside the storm battered on, thunder booming through the empty bar while the rain furiously hammered the roof.

"I don't want to be alone," she said, defeated.

JP smiled, remembering Sly's talk about not being afraid of being alone; he made Bridget a stiff drink.

"Don't be, because right now you're not alone."

"You know what I mean," she pouted. "I feel like a nobody."

"Don't be," he reiterated and slid her the Long Island iced tea. "When you aren't afraid of being alone, you won't feel that way anymore. You'll feel like a somebody."

Bridget looked at him with an odd mix of emotions on her face. Then she grabbed the Long Island iced tea and took a long drink.

# CHAPTER 19

# A Someone

---

The next morning Bridget was woken harshly by her alarm. She had spent an unhealthy amount of the previous night awake, pondering everything that she had heard, felt, and thought yesterday. Now that morning had come, it was time to put those thoughts away and focus on the day at hand.

Today she was filling in for a middle school English teacher in one of the suburbs. It was an easy assignment. Middle school was her favorite because the kids were old enough to actually be taught, but young enough to still be intimidated if she had to do it.

She made breakfast and went to the bedroom to get dressed. As she scanned her closest, however, she concluded that she had nothing to wear. Standing there and pouting for a bit, she tried to figure out how she felt. She sighed in frustration, but immediately after, she got an idea. Maybe if she dressed like she felt great, she might actually start to feel better. She went straight to the back of the closet and spied a dress she hadn't worn in a long time. It was a little snug, but boy did it make her look good. She almost wore heels, but decided that stilettos might be a bit too risqué for middle school, so she settled on her favorite pair of boots.

When she finished dressing and putting on her make-up, she packed her lunch and left, realizing she'd be lucky if she showed up on-time, much less early like she was supposed to be.

She arrived a few minutes before the start-of-day bell would ring, and got to her classroom to set up. Suddenly, she heard a knock at the door.

"Good morning," the knocker said, entering. "I'm Mr. Santi, I'm the other seventh grade English teacher."

"Oh, hello," Bridget said, standing up a little awkwardly, straightening her dress out. She was pleasantly surprised to see that his eyes immediately drew down and then back up her person, and she did the same to him. He was quite the tall drink of water. He had a full head of dark hair, with the same colored mustache and a full beard. He was very tall and clearly very fit, and he looked very sharp with his khakis and a long-sleeve button-up of deep purple.

"I'm, Bridget, er, uh, Ms. Young," she said a bit uneasily, standing just in front of the desk as he walked over to shake her hand. She smiled and continued, "I'm still not used to introducing myself by my last name. I haven't been sub teaching very long."

"Ha, I understand," he said jovially. "Then call me Liam, Bridget." They shook hands and then he straightened himself up a bit before continuing, "I just wanted to pop in real quick and see if there was anything I could help you with before class started."

"Oh, I, uh," Bridget began, recollecting herself. She need to find an excuse to keep him here. He had his hands in his pockets and she really wanted to see if he had a ring on his finger. "I, uh, I think I need a little help with the electronic board here." That was not true, every public school these days had electronic boards, and she had picked up how to use it during her first assignment.

"Ah, of course, they can be temperamental," Liam said, reaching up with his left hand and powering it on; Bridget's stomach gave a little jump as his hand was unadorned. He then went on to explain how to turn it on and off, as well as how to alternate settings between slideshow and editing mode.

"Thank you so much," Bridget fawned despite knowing all of that already. "You were so helpful."

"My pleasure," Liam said. "The bell's about to ring, but if you need other help or anything else this morning, just stop in next door."

"I certainly will," Bridget said as Liam waved to her as he exited. She took a deep breath as she sat down, her heart fluttering a bit.

That morning went by very well, with most of the students well-behaved if inattentive; Mr. Santi stopped by again over lunch to see if all was well and Bridget claimed to be having some trouble with the school wifi, which he was more than happy to assist her with. He wound up sticking around for a decent portion of the lunch period, and the two talked and laughed. A few hours later, the end of day bell rang and she stepped out into the hallway to help monitor the kids as they went to their lockers. Mr. Santi was standing near his door as she did, but when he saw her, he walked over to her door.

"So how did the day go, Ms. Young?" he asked.

"Really well, actually," she said, smiling. "The kids were actually as good as advertised." They shared a laugh at that.

"That's good to hear," Mr. Santi said. "So, have you taught here before?"

"Yes. Well no," she answered. "I subbed for a day at the high school last week, but never here at the middle school."

"I see. How far away do you live that you sub here?"

"I live in the city, so it's only twenty minutes down 794."

"Oh, that's not bad at all," Mr. Santi said. "So you live in the city?"

"Yeah, just off Brady Street," she replied.

"Oh, no kidding. I love going to this pizza joint in the city near Cathedral Square, Wetzel's. Have you ever been there?"

"No, I haven't been inside, but I know where it is," she said. It was true, she had walked past it many a summer night when she had gone out to the bars near Cathedral Square.

"Oh, the pizza is to die for," Mr. Santi said, waving his head in emphasis. "I'd love to take you there sometime. What are you up to this Friday?"

She was more than a bit shocked by Mr. Santi's straightforwardness, but she was by no means disappointed. While she had been flirting with him all day, she hadn't expected him to make such an assertive move on her. She could feel her heart fluttering again.

"Uh, nothing I can think of," she answered, realizing she had paused awkwardly long.

"Then let's do dinner Friday evening after school at Wetzel's," he said with a smile, more a statement than a question.

While her heart was still aflutter, she had enough sense of mind to give a faux hesitation before she answered, "Yes, that would be wonderful."

\* \* \* \* \*

Friday night arrived and Bridget was equally extremely excited and palpably nervous. She was so excited to be going on a date. She arrived a few minutes late, insurance so that she wouldn't be there alone waiting for Liam. She had decided not to change up the formula that had clearly gotten his eye the day they had met, so she went with her old sweater dress that fit a little too snug (not as bad, now that she had lost a few pounds since moving out on her own) and a pair of heeled boots this time. As she walked inside, she found him right away at a small, square table. He stood up when he saw her and beckoned her over; when she arrived he gave her a hug and a greeting, then pulled the chair to his left out and ushered her to sit. Just before she sat, she made sure to pause so that he could drink in her outfit, which she happily noticed that he did.

The evening was the most fun Bridget had since she had started her life on her own again. Liam was polite, chivalrous, well-mannered, asked about her at every opportunity, and was unafraid to talk about himself in palatable portions. Most surprising of all, he seemed to have none of the nerves that she had going into this date. After they had both finished eating and the check had arrived, he steadfastly refused to let her even touch it. As he placed his card in the slot, he cracked a joke with the waiter, which all three of them enjoyed.

Bridget could not deny that she was totally surprised with and impressed by him. He was so at ease with her and himself; he loved to write, that was why he was an English teacher, and had even published some short stories; he was a football and track coach at the high school; he even found time to volunteer at a food pantry on Saturday mornings, something she told him she could see herself doing with him in the next couple of weekends. She was amazed by him, so much so she had to say something.

"Liam," she began, "I have just had so much fun tonight. You really know how to treat a lady, and you seem so passionate about everything you're doing."

He laughed cordially as she said that. "Oh, you're too kind. I'm nothing special, I'm just another someone." His sentence forced her ears to perk up; she was frozen by his quip about anybody.

"No," she smiled to herself, wondering what JP would say if he could hear what she was about to say. "No, you are *someone*, that's why you're special."

He gave a small laugh at her remark and thanked her.

Bridget was almost floating. She wasn't sure her smile left her face until she heard, "Should we get going?" to which she could only smile and nod.

"Let me walk you to your car," he said.

"Oh, you don't have to," she answered.

"That wasn't a question," he replied with a warm smile. The two walked out and Bridget tried to loosen up as they did. She had parked down the hill towards the river a couple blocks. As they started their descent, he extended his elbow for her to take, which she gratefully did; even though she loved heels and boots and was actually pretty smooth in them, any sort of incline or decline was no friend to any girl in heels.

They got to her car and he walked over to the driver-side door and waited for her to unlock it. Just after she did, he reached out and put his arms around her.

"Thank you for a great night," he said simply, staring into her eyes with a smile. "You look wonderful."

"Thank you," she said, her smile flashing excitement. "I had a wonderful time myself." He started leaning into her, his lips getting closer and closer to hers. She barely debated whether to give in to him or not before surrendering to the part of her that wanted this as much as he did. Their lips met and locked together. It was scintillating. She felt herself get swept up in the tides of carnal passion, the both of them suddenly holding each other closer and tighter, their bodies pressed together, their lips in a dance that made her heart pump like it hadn't in years. Bridget heard a car horn honk, but she gave it no notice, nor did Liam. The two kissed long and passionately.

After what felt like both hours and moments, they both released each other, and quickly gasped for a breath of air.

"Wow," Liam said, a huge smile on his face.

"Wow," Bridget said. The two leaned their heads together as they regrouped. After some time, Liam released her and opened the door for her.

"Have good night, Bridget," he said as she stepped aside to let her in.

"You, too, Liam," she said, turning to smile at him one last time. As she did, he leaned over the door and kissed her tenderly on the cheek. She smiled again and winked at him as she climbed into her car. Then he closed it and started walking away. Through the rear-view mirror she could see him turn and look back at her.

She smiled to herself and let out a giddy scream. It had been the best possible night she could've hoped for. He was a gentleman, a scholar, a teacher, a writer, a poet, and a lover; he was indeed *someone* as he had said. Then she paused. Someone. That line started to ring in her ears again.

In an instant, however, her whole manner changed. She suddenly felt a horrible revelation dawn on her, one that gave her a physical chill down her spine: he was, indeed, a *someone*, but she was not. Here he was, confidant and unafraid of life by himself, embracing every aspect of being single. He was doing so many things with his time, he had so many passions and dreams. He was pursuing so many things with his life, and he had already achieved many more.

Starkly contrasting that, was Bridget. Bridget, who had over the past seven months had to completely start from scratch because she had been lured astray by false passions; by her own lies, as Sly had told her. Here she was in the midst of the most tumultuous period in her life, and here was the most exceptional person she had ever met. Well, one of the most exceptional people.

JP's words echoed within her again: 'When you aren't afraid of being alone, you won't feel that way anymore, you'll feel like a somebody.'

She realized that right there, it made no difference in the world to her if Liam was the most amazing guy in the world or not, this wouldn't be right. It didn't matter if she started dating him, got engaged to him, or married him, she would be no different than she was with Ryan. Sure, her situation around her would different, but she would be the same person, still afraid of being alone. Liam wasn't afraid of being alone, he seemed to savor it. It wasn't that he had achieved his dreams, it's that he had them, and was working toward them. That's why he wasn't afraid of being alone, she realized. But her? If she started dating him, any moment she couldn't be with him, she would feel anxious and sad. She wasn't like that, she wasn't *someone*.

Feeling lost and confused, she turned the car on and decided she needed to go for a long drive and think.

\* \* \* \* \*

Meanwhile, some ninety miles south, Sly sat in an old Irish bar—Murray's—that he had sat in many times before; this was always his first stop during his trips south of the state line. Now he sat there again, the once casual bar was a bustling scene of nightlife with live music and dancing, host to all manner of people: college kids, young professionals, and locals of the high-end, expensive condos.

As he sat there, sipping his beer and looking around, he studied the various people there. As he scanned from person to person, his eyes came to rest on a young woman, just out of college, if he had to guess. She clearly had eyes for him, and he had gotten very good at picking out the people who seemed to have eyes for him. As she glanced from him to her friends, the crowd parted a bit, and he was a bit taken aback when he saw her outfit: a leather mini-skirt and stiletto heels. Bridget's favorite outfit for going out.

Suddenly she walked away from her friends and started toward the bar, angling towards Sly. She seemed like she was going to pass by him, but she took an awkward step and fell into him.

"Oh my gosh, I'm so sorry!" she cried, purposefully flailing on him. He politely pushed her back up.

"Not a big deal," Sly muttered, trying to turn her off.

"Oh my gosh, thank you so much!" she exclaimed. "I don't know what happened, that was *sooo* weird." He waved it off, cringing at her emphasis on 'so'. "I'm Crystal," she said, sliding close to him.

"Sly," he said without looking.

She leaned in between him and the bar, trying to puff her chest towards him. "That's a sexy name. Do you come here often, Sly?" she asked, satisfied with his view of her cleavage.

"No," he said bluntly, trying to send her a message.

"That's too bad," she said, sliding her hip on the side of his leg. "It would've been great to meet you before." She suddenly took a step up on the bar's footrest and placed herself squarely on his lap,

"Get off!" he roared, pushing her off his lap, standing up and pushing his stool back so he could get her further away from him. She tumbled into another guy at the bar, who stood up and took a fighting stance as he faced Sly.

"Hey!" she cried, Sly's actions already having drawn the attention of the bartender and the people nearby. "You don't have to be such a dick! I'm just trying to be friendly."

He could feel a fury rising inside of him, an unbridled rage that he had not experienced in many years. Just trying to be friendly? He tensed up, ready to tell her what he really thought of her. Before he could, however, he felt a large hand on his shoulder.

"We don't need any of that around here," a man, clearly the bouncer, said. "You'll have to get drinks somewhere else the rest of the night."

Sly nodded and allowed himself to be escorted to the exit. Once he was outside the bar, he took a long look around him. He used to love this city, this city of a million blinding lights; the sights, the sounds, the feel. This city was the place he had slowly learned to love when he had worked down here, and it was the place he always envisioned himself meeting someone he could share the rest of his life with. Now he had returned with no such ambitions. He realized the old love he had for this city was all an illusion.

Behind the lights and before the storefronts, the city was a wounded thing, a bleeding creature. While he had lived here in the light of the day, he had seen only the best parts. But, ironically, strangely, in the darkness of his perpetual night he had begun to see the suffering side of the city. He saw the parts and people that everyone—residents, students, tourists—all averted their eyes from: the crime, the homelessness, the sick, the suffering. All things people wanted to turn their eyes away from, pretend they didn't exist. It was sickening to Sly. He silently hated himself for once being one of those people.

At a loss for anything else to do, he started walking down the street, heading to the lakefront. It was warm, and people were out and about all over. As he walked, various people passed by him: an older couple, a group of college kids, a bachelorette party, a young couple; all of them happy to ignore him. Sly felt resentment toward them bubbling up in him. He carried on, and as he did, he passed some different people now: homeless men and women. No one other than him seemed to acknowledge these wretched people. These people were just like him: invisible, forgotten.

He carried on through the night, completely alone. Before he was afflicted with his condition, he used to love the night. He would stand in the window of his high-rise apartment in downtown and look out over the world, wondering about his life and the story it might one day be. He used to envision a future with a wife and children, of him becoming the CEO of his company, of him retiring somewhere warm and luxurious. Maybe he would write a book, maybe he would travel, maybe he would become wealthy enough to become a philanthropist. He used to love the night. Now he hated it because the night was what took all of that from him.

He paused at an intersection and looked up at the tall buildings around him. He wondered how many of them loved the night, loved looking out over the city, dreaming. Few, if any, he decided. Then he realized that these people were invisible, too. Not like him or the homeless people—people invisible by circumstance. No, these people were invisible by choice, but in a completely different way.

These were people like Bridget, people who were terrified to be alone, terrified of confronting the fact that they were not living or striving for their dreams. Instead of being their own person they had fallen in line with the voice of the world. The voice of the world told them that not being happy and satisfied was a disease, a pariah. The voice that said if you your dreams were too hard to reach, dilute them and diminish them to make them achievable. These people were invisible in the sense that rather than live their own lives, they pursued the things they were told would make them happy: going out to the bars, following the shows and trends popular with everyone else, constantly checking and re-checking social media. Anything to fit it, anything to avoid having a quiet moment. While Sly had always run towards the night—towards those quiet moments—everyone else ran from the night, away from those quiet moments. They didn't realize that to be alone—to have a quiet moment—was to dream.

As long as there were people running from the night, afraid to be alone, there would be people like him. And not just a steady number, but a constantly growing number. JP had always referred to their condition as a sickness, but Sly had never been comfortable with that term; now, however, he fully understood. His and JP's condition was not the sickness of the night, that primal fear of being alone was. That fear was the first symptom, and—given enough time and enough opportunities—the same condition Sly had would affect them. There were dozens of people like him. How long would it be until he encountered hundreds? How long until he encountered thousands? How long until everyone in the world lived incurably in the night?

The thought sickened him. Between him and JP, he had been the optimistic one, believing that one day they might find a cure for his condition; not a work-around like when Bridget stayed up all night with him, but a true cure, a way to truly escape the night. Now, however, he was beginning to think differently.

# CHAPTER 20

# Dawn and Dusk

———————

Bridget was dreaming. It was a pleasant dream. She was sitting in the front yard of a house, her house, enjoying the sunshine of a warm summer's day. But there was this ringing and buzzing that seemed to be echoing through it. Trapped in a lucid state for what felt like forever, she finally realized that her phone was ringing in the real world. Her eyes shot open and she reached over and grabbed it, answering without bothering to look at who was calling.

"Hello?" she asked.

"Good morning, Bridget," she heard Liam's voice proclaim.

"Oh, ah, good morning, Liam," she answered, straightening up in bed subconsciously. She looked her clock. It was almost noon! She recalled briefly how the previous night she had been unable to sleep, her mind turning over and over again continuously until exhaustion finally claimed her.

Liam and Bridget echoed how much fun they both had the previous evening before Liam went on to say he had a buddy who was playing a set at a local hipster bar that coming Wednesday and then extended her an offer to join him. She said that sounded like a lot of fun, but her Wednesday was booked. Liam said it was no problem, and then said simply that he looked forward to seeing her again. She parroted him and they said their good-byes.

As she hung up the phone, she put her hands over her face and lay back down.

As great as Liam was, and as wonderful as she imagined life could be with him, she had realized that chasing him now would be a mistake. While she wanted to pursue a relationship with Liam, it would be the opposite of what she needed to do. Right now, the thing she needed to do was confront her deepest, most sincere desires, and then pursue them. With that in mind, she got out of bed and made breakfast.

As the day wore on, she started writing down all the things that came to mind: being a teacher, living in the city, falling in love, getting really fit, learning to knit, photography, the piano. As nighttime came she finally sat down with all of what she had written and came to conclusion: leaving Ryan—while difficult—had been the first real step toward pursuing her dreams. While living all alone in a tiny, month-to-month apartment as a substitute teacher was decidedly not her dream, she was definitely farther along on the road than she had ever been before.

As she sat there, she stole a glance outside her window. The leaves were rustling in the evening breeze, and through her window she heard the shouts and calls of Brady Street as it came alive in the night. She wondered what all those people's lives were like. She pushed her desk chair closer to the window and continued to listen for a while. The more she listened, however, the more she began to imagine her own future doing all these things she had written down. She smiled to herself.

In that moment, she realized that while she had lost so much to get to this point, she was happier for it. While it had been difficult to give up so many things she once held dear, it was worth it if only to be able to chase her dreams again.

As she looked out and saw the last traces of the sun setting, she realized that a new day was dawning in her life. She wondered what Sly would say to her if she could talk to him now.

*   *   *   *   *

Sly watched from the sidewalk circling the planetarium as the first light of dawn began to trace the night sky. This had been his favorite spot to go to when he worked in the city. From that peninsula he could see the whole city before him, shimmering. Now as he stood atop the steps of the planetarium, he stared at the glowing city. He recalled the quote he had held so dear all these years, that if you loved until it hurt, there would be no more hurt, only love.

The world was full of hurt, lonely people, people who would try to find solace to ease their pain, by running from it, or internalizing it, or—worst of all—lashing out and hurting others. He remembered another quote he had heard: hurt people hurt people. In a world so full of hurt and loneliness, how could there be room for love?

Sly bowed his head and put his head in his hands, shaking it. Hurt and pain were spreading over the world, and there was nothing he could do about it. Just like his disease, there was nothing that he could do to stop or cure it. Pain and loneliness, the two things that would slowly, inexorably, drag people into the night where, one-by-one, they would become invisible and forgotten. If this pain could not be stopped, if this cycle could not be broken, then surely his condition would afflict the world over.

He watched as the first light of dawn penetrated the sky and knew that he only had moments before he would blink into the next night. He silently wondered if this was the beginning of the end, the dusk of humanity. He shed a tear at the thought of a whole world of people like himself, people trapped in the night.

# CHAPTER 21

# The Flint and the Steel

───────────

Bridget was both very excited and a little upset with herself. Here she was, about to have a get-together with her new coworkers on Brady Street, and she was completely ready to go with over an hour until she needed to leave. She sighed to herself with a small laugh. She was out of practice with this sort of thing.

The first week of classes at her new school had just finished up, and while she hadn't done much teaching, she was in desperate need of a strong drink and good times. She decided to help organize a get-together, a way to loosen up a bit outside of their work setting. She tried to remember the last time she had gone out with her friends, and concluded that it had been when Kim had gotten engaged in February.

Speaking of Kim's wedding, she needed to mail back her RSVP soon; Kim and her fiancé had a date set for next spring. Bridget decided to fill it out right there and drop it in the public mailbox on the corner on her way to the bar. She checked the box for chicken dinner and absentmindedly marked the RSVP down just for herself, no plus-one. She decided to give it a quick review, but this time her eyes lingered on the empty box for plus-one. She had an introspective moment as she realized that a year ago she would never have dared to send in a wedding RSVP for just herself.

In the past year so much had happened that she felt like the life she led now was completely apart from her old life with Ryan. The first day of this new life began when she told Liam that while he was the greatest guy she had ever met, she was a hot mess, and unready for a relationship. Seeing him had given her a vision of sorts to strive for. While he was reasonably upset, he told her that he understood and wished her the best.

After that, she finished up her licensure program, applied for full-time teaching gigs, and got a job at a middle school that she had subbed at the previous school year. Also in the past year, she had taken up photography as a hobby, her favorite time to shoot being at night. On the summer nights she wasn't taking photographs, she was helping JP tend the bar at Mike's to keep the money coming in. Her bank account was a lot slimmer these days, but so was she. She had started riding her bike for workouts, and she would spend hours biking all along the lakefront.

Of all the things that had changed, one thing that hadn't was her apartment. While it was kind of cramped and definitely wasn't the nicest place around, it was clean and she had made it her home. Her walls were now adorned with her own photography, and she had gotten rid of lots of things that she didn't need or use anymore. In line with that notion, her wardrobe had been greatly simplified. While she had always liked dressing for attention and to be cute, she had learned that when someone paid attention to her clothing, they weren't paying attention to her. Gone was the sweater dress that didn't fit, gone the leather skirt that Ryan loved so much. Gone was anything that she didn't need or enjoy wearing for the comfort of it.

Bridget caught herself looking in the mirror as she thought about Kim and her coming wedding. Then she laughed to herself as she saw what she was wearing: a flowy, sleeveless summer dress of brilliant yellow. This was exactly how Kim would dress when the girls would all go out. Now Bridget understood why Kim had dressed like this; it was really comfortable.

"What a year," she said out loud, looking up from her desk out her window. She could hear the ruckus of Brady Street on a Friday night starting up, and as she listened, memories began to flow back to her of how she had gotten herself in this position, of the man who started this journey—ironically—by rebuffing Kim's flirtatious efforts.

Oh, Sly. Bridget had so many things she wanted to tell him now, so many things to show him and explain to him. Sure he was gone, but she was certain that he would be back one day. Then she wondered when that day came, would she be ready? Surely not, she could probably fill a book with everything she wanted to tell him; she would have to write it all down. She looked at the clock again, a smile curling on the edge of her lips. She made a bold decision.

She walked over to her desk and grabbed a few pieces of paper and her best pen. Sitting down, she started penning a letter to Sly, one that she could not be certain he would ever see. . .

When she was finally finished writing, she had scribbled through several sheets of paper and over an hour had passed. She gasped at how long she had been writing, then rushed out to Brady Street to meet up with her fellow teachers.

Right from the start, Bridget could tell it was going to be a good night. She met up with the early birds at a hole-in-the-wall joint that—from the minute she walked in—she was wondering how she had never stepped in there before. As others showed up, the night really began: dancing, chatting, drinking—it was all a blast. She took in her time with these new coworkers with absolute pleasure.

As the night wore on, a week of early mornings started to hit everyone, and they started heading out even before 9:00. Bridget, fresh off working nights all summer at Mike's, stayed out until even the few teachers that remained finally left for home. Bridget followed the last of her coworkers out before starting back to her place.

She smiled as she walked through the raucous streets alone, the full bacchanalia of Brady Street in its prime: the cars blocking the street, the music blasting from the bars, the warm, humid evening of early September. She tried to remember the last time she had gone out like this. As she rounded the corner for home, she suddenly felt like a night on Brady without stopping in at Mike's would be a waste, a shame. Maybe Sly would be there this time . . .

She stopped suddenly and looked down at the sidewalk. She had been having that thought a lot lately. She felt a little bad about it, then told herself that if she was going to Mike's, it had to be to visit JP, not to hope and wish that Sly were there. A smile crept over her face as she shook her head. Going to a bar and hoping to meet a guy there. Old habits die hard, she supposed.

Over at Mike's, things had been a little slow. The live music that had been promised never showed up, so JP had to refund everyone's cover charge and a lot of people partook in the exodus to a more happening part of Brady Street. The crowd had just cleared out and things seemed like they would fall into a rut for a while, maybe lasting the entire night. JP had been a bartender long enough to know that a slow night rarely picked up after a crowd of people cleared out.

He looked to the front door and his mouth dropped open as he saw who was walking into the bar.

"Welcome back, you old dog," JP said, a big smile appearing on his face.

"Hey, JP," Sly said, forcing a smile at his old friend.

JP walked out to the other side of the bar and he and Sly shared a hug.

"How've you been?" JP asked, placing his hands on Sly's shoulders as they parted.

Sly gave an exhausted sigh for his response. JP stared at Sly concernedly as he walked back behind the bar. JP poured a drink of his favorite local stein.

"How was the big city?" JP asked, more than a little off-put by Sly's pouty demeanor.

Sly sighed again before he spoke. "Ugly."

JP gave Sly a look as if to ask what that meant.

"After a while of living life like we have," Sly continued, slouching a bit in his seat "you begin to see just how ugly and beaten and terrible life is. How broken so many people's lives are, not just ours. When all you see is the darkness, you learn just how many things everyone hides in it."

JP nodded. What was with Sly tonight? Sly had always been the guardedly optimistic one, while JP had been the healthy cynic. The tables seemed to have turned now. JP caught himself realizing that spending a whole summer working with Bridget had made him a more optimistic individual, although he would never admit it to her. "You saw a lot of darkness." JP said. "Did you see any light?"

Sly shook his head as he slumped onto the bar. "No," he said simply. "I didn't. I'm not even sure it exists anymore."

JP paused as Sly say this. "Hey, man, you and I both have seen a lot of darkness. What happened to you being a beacon of light in the darkness like that dome with the light you saw, that seminary?"

Sly shook his head. "No one can be a light forever. Given enough time, every fire eventually burns out. So too does the human spirit."

"Yours doesn't have to be burnt out," JP tried to reason. Suddenly he felt a rush of wind blow through the bar as someone came in through the back door. "A strong wind can reignite ashes."

"There are no ashes, there is no fire," Sly snapped at him.

"Then you just need a spark," JP began, suddenly smiling as he saw who had entered through the back door. "The steel just needs to meet the flint."

Sly was about to give JP a piece of his mind when he heard a voice from the past call his name. "Sly?"

Bridget was standing there, her heart racing. Was it really him? "Sly?" she asked again.

He said nothing, but Bridget saw the smile on JP's face and hurried over to grab the stool next to Sly.

"Hello, Bridget," he said without turning.

"Oh, my gosh," she started, short on breath. "I had this thought you would be here tonight. Oh my gosh, I'm so happy to see you again. It's been so long."

"When was the last time you looked for me?" Sly asked condescendingly, disbelieving that she had ever really been waiting for him.

She answered without hesitation. "Last Friday. And the Friday before that, and every week of the last year."

Sly sat up and looked at JP to see if he would corroborate her story, which he did with a simple, smiling nod. "She helped me run the place all summer."

Sly had not expected that response. He said nothing as he sipped his drink.

Bridget broke the silence by asking, "Were you in–?"

"Chicago," Sly answered bluntly.

"Why did you go there?" she asked.

"Because I had overstayed my visit here."

Bridget felt the barb of that remark. It was meant for her, that pointed comment, and she knew it. She had driven him away, and she knew it.

"And I'm just passing through now," Sly said.

Bridget wanted to ask why, she wanted to know why he was like this, what had happened to him in Chicago. She very nearly asked why, but instead, she found herself making a statement instead of a question.

"You know," she began, "for a guy seeking permanence, that seems fleeting."

JP pursed his lips and exhaled in pleasant surprise at Bridget's feistiness. Sly sat up straight and turned to her, his patience clearly at its limit, but also perplexed by her remark. Bridget stood there in proud defiance, not backing down from what she had just said.

"I've learned better now. I used to be an optimist. Now I'm a realist. I have a clearer picture of reality this time around," Sly explained.

"How can you–?" Bridget started, but Sly spoke over her.

"Nothing in this world is permanent," he declared in his own infallibly. "My condition hasn't made it that way for me, it's like that for everyone all the same. I used to think I could escape this one day. Having lived in the darkness as long as I have, I know better now. Nothing is permanent in this world, and our inevitable deaths are the proof of that."

Bridget was stunned by what she was hearing. Who was this man?

Sly paused and hung his head as he continued. "I used to think true love was permanent. I used to think it was a beautiful thing that could be infinite, eternal, flawless. Love means giving everything to another person, being willing to go so far as to give up your own life. I used to think that it was possible for love to be so perfect that there would be no more hurt, only love. I don't believe that such a thing exists anymore."

Sly drained the rest of his beer as JP and Bridget gave each other a glance of shock and horror. Then he continued.

"Maybe it existed at some point in some bygone era of poets and romantics, but not today. Everyone is too selfish, too arrogant. How many relationships really reach a point where they give everything? None of them. No one is really willing to give up everything. Love was always purely idealized and held up as an impossible standard, a foolish hope as an opium for the hopeless. If ever a fire of love burned in this world, the only way we will ever know is by sifting through its ashes."

Sly finished and, though it didn't seem possible, he actually slumped harder against the bar, a truly broken man.

Bridget had no idea what to say. This was not the Sly she had known so long ago. He was a shadow of the man he used to be, of the man she had grown to know. For all the times she had come to him with her problems, he had never spoken first, he had always let her tell her part. This time he had spoken first. This time he was here spilling his problems to her.

It was her time to share everything she had learned and realized through him. The memory of everything in her letter resounded loud and clear in her mind.

"You can't find love," she started, her voice feeling very small again, "because maybe it has to find you."

Sly sat up, stunned by her response. "What?" JP smiled like he had never smiled before.

"You-you," she began slowly, unsure how he would respond to her now that their roles were reversed. "You used to tell me that love is a two-way street. Of course you can't find it alone, it takes two people."

Sly sat up, a puzzled look on his face.

Bridget continued, feeling empowered. "You keep talking about love as this thing that only involves giving. Love is a sacrifice, and yes, a sacrifice involves giving. But you sacrifice *for something*, not just to lose things. Sacrifice also involves getting something back.

"I've sacrificed a lot this last year, since you left. I've sacrificed my job, my apartment, my fiancé, everything. Everything about me is different now. I've done it for something that I love—just as you told me I might: teaching. I love teaching, I love being a teacher. And I do so many things now that I love that I never would've done in my old life. I get so much joy and happiness out of photography, and riding my bike, and working here all summer, and just being comfortable being myself. I sacrificed a lot for my own happiness—to be *someone*. And I've never been happier."

Sly was sitting up even further, staring at Bridget as if he couldn't believe what he was hearing.

"Love isn't about giving, it's about sharing. Your mistake, Sly," she pointed at him, "was to look for someone who would be willing to *take away* your sufferings. But rather, you should've been looking for someone who would be willing to *share* your sufferings."

Sly was sitting totally erect at this point, his mouth open a little bit as he stared at Bridget.

Bridget hung her head as she spoke again. "Every day since you asked me, I have kept within my heart and pondered your question. Every day I revisit the question that you, rightfully, scolded me for lying to you about: would I take your burden? The day you asked me the answer was clearly no, even though I denied it. I didn't know any better. But at some point in the past year, I've come to believe that yes, yes I would take your burden. Not out of pity or some sense of self-righteousness. No, I would take it out of love."

Bridget heard her own voice and sighed. She realized in that moment she would've done that for the Sly she knew before he left. But since they had last seen each other, he had changed as much as she did, and in the worst ways.

"At least, I was willing to take it. . . for the man I once knew."

A long silence ensued, and Bridget and Sly sat alone. The silence filled the bar while Brady Street partied on completely ignorant of the drama within this single bar. Slowly, Bridget realized that no one else was there, the music was quiet, and it was only Sly, JP and her. She looked about frantically, then saw JP smile, nod, and wink at her; he had closed the bar shortly after she began her piece.

Sly, however, noticed none of these things. He was contemplating all she had told him, carefully measuring each of her words. After a very, very long silence, he found the strength and will to speak.

"I'm sorry, Bridget," he said, staring into her eyes apologetically. "It's hard to see the light when you live in darkness."

She smiled.

He continued. "You're right. About everything you just said. I'm just. . . I don't know what to say."

Bridget smiled as she saw a glimpse of the old Sly beneath his new, coarse exterior.

"Well," she began, "that would be a first."

JP suddenly broke out into laughter, a hearty, full laughter. Bridget started to giggle at him, never having seen him so happy.

"That's enough," Sly muttered, the ends of his mouth turning up. But JP laughed and laughed. Bridget joined him, too, and then even Sly found himself chuckling.

After a few blissful minutes of laughter, a somber silence returned. No one seemed to know what to say at this point.

In that moment, Bridget knew the time had come. "I know," she began, her emotion beginning to surge around her. "I know that I can never take your burden from you. But I am willing to share it with you."

JP and Sly each gave a jolt of shock, both of them understanding what she meant: that she would willingly contract this sickness of the night.

"That's not an easy burden to carry, living only in the night," Sly said in quiet awe. "I would only agree with it if you would agree to be married. And even then only once we were actually married. And I know that you never really wanted–"

"I agree," she said with a straightforward smile. She knew he was going to say something about how she had never wanted to get married. She had changed many beliefs over the past year, and this was one of them.

"We can't just get married right away like this," Sly said. "We can't just rush into this. This condition is not an easy commitment."

Bridget smiled as she replied, "Neither is marriage."

# CHAPTER 22

# The Morning

---

That night at Mike's on Brady, Sly and Bridget made an agreement about something that had never been done before: that someone might willingly enter the night. They made a pledge to be open and honest about anything and everything: their fears, their feelings, their thoughts, their desires. Finally, they made it clear that if after one year Bridget still felt these feelings and desires to share the night with Sly, they would be wed.

The next few months were some of the most exciting and exhausting in Bridget's life. There was a period of adjustment that was difficult on Bridget. Not only was she working all day and trying to continue her photography and biking, but now she was seeing a man who could only be seen at or after her normal bedtime. Given their situations, they could not meet every day, and they refused to do so. While they desired to be together, if love was patient, so must they be.

Over time, they started spending more and more sleepless nights together, always out in the night or at home in the warm embrace of Bridget's apartment. The first time Bridget showed Sly to her apartment, he realized it was the exact same one he had lived in. On the nights they didn't stay in, they often stopped in at Mike's, visiting with JP.

The next spring, Bridget and Sly tried something very daring: going to Kim's wedding together. It was in the city, and they reckoned if they stuck with the crowd, there was no way Sly would disappear. Bridget got up just before sunrise to meet Sly, and the two held hands almost incessantly all day; Bridget got some unpleasant looks about it, but at this point she didn't care what others thought about them, no one else know the truth.

The wedding was a beautiful ceremony. Steph sat near Bridget and Sly, and kept passing knowing glances to Bridget about Sly. Bridget merely smiled back when she did this. Of all her friends, Steph was the one she might one day confide in if the time ever came. That day—for the first time since she was a child—Bridget had visions of herself dressed in white, with friends and family in attendance, watching her walking down the aisle. By the time they had to go, Bridget had wondered how she had ever not wanted to be married.

The school year started to wind down, and they were spending more and more nights together, even some days, as Bridget would get up early to meet Sly. On those early mornings, they would go watch the sunrise in the park together like they had their first morning. By the time summer came, it wasn't too uncommon for them to show up at Mike's in the early evening, having spent the entire day together. A hazard that they found with this, however, was that if Bridget was not supremely attentive to Sly, he would disappear on her when she least expected it.

On one particularly fine and beautiful sunrise in late-June, Sly proposed to Bridget. She gave an unequivocal and fearless yes. After that, she informed the school she taught at that she would be leaving that job for personal reasons. Her and Sly agreed to be married in early September, and they agreed to make it a private ceremony, the two of them and JP. They set the venue at the church Bridget had started going to on Sundays just down the street from Mike's.

\* \* \* \* \*

It was there, at that small church on a cool fall evening that they were wed. I was so proud to be their best man and primary witness. It was a wonderful ceremony. And then that night, they consummated their marriage and Bridget entered into the night, the first and only person to ever willingly do so. After that, they never looked back.

A year of wedded bliss they had, and together they shared the purest joy. It was beautiful and inspiring. They discovered that if they both remained with each other during the days that they could live in the sun. However, there were many instances when they found themselves basking in the glory of the day only to blink into the night. In time, they got better, and soon they were spending so many days awake that they decided to try and find a place together. Sly checked on his investments and stocks for the first time in years, and they found they had enough money to keep the small apartment Bridget had leased. They even decided to get a little more spending money by helping me pull a few shifts at Mike's.

Then, on Christmas Eve in the second year of their marriage, they returned to Mike's with a story that would change everything.

It was the morning of the 23rd, the first morning after the winter solstice, the first morning after the longest night of the year. They had been getting all of their loose ends tied off, because they were going to travel across the country together. Milwaukee had gotten too small for them, they claimed. The whole night was theirs, why stay confined to one place?

But that particular morning, something happened. They had some library books to return and a rent check to drop off before they left on their grand adventure. The sunrise was none-too-far off, Sly suggested they each take one task and reconvene that evening. After all, they wouldn't be leaving until night fall, when they could be sure they wouldn't blink out of their car in the middle of the day on the freeway.

The sky was beginning to turn gold as Sly slid the overdue books into the library slot and Bridget deposited the check in the safety deposit box outside the landlord's residence across the river. They started walking back to the apartment as the sky grew lighter and lighter. They were surprised to see they were still walking in the daylight.

They finally returned to their apartment with the sun decidedly risen, and they both wondered to each other what was going on. Somewhat afraid, they started to try different things that would work to get them to blink into the night. They stood facing away from each other and remained as silent as they could, but every time they tried that, they still remained there. Sly went into the bathroom while Bridget went into the closet, but they still remained there.

It took them the rest of the day to realize one unbelievable conclusion: they were free of the night.

That night they went to bed in Bridget's tiny twin bed and woke up the next day, shocked to still be there. For the first time in forever, they both felt tired and hungry, and Sly had to go to the bathroom for the first time in years.

They didn't understand it at the time, but over the next few weeks and days, I was the one that came to understand and, finally, had something to teach them.

Those two had found that ideal, authentic love, the entire sharing *of* each other *for* each other. They had come to care so deeply for the other that there was never a moment where they were unseen, unheard, unfelt, unwanted, or unloved. They were no longer sick and broken people, but rather, together they had found wholeness.

The love they shared was not just a feeling, it was a choice. It was a call that they each took up, a call to care as much for each other as themselves. And they succeeded. In so doing, they cured themselves of their sickness of the night and rejoined the people of the sun. They had escaped the darkness.

Love is a miracle, and their love was the proof of that. The ability to care for someone more than ourselves, that's a miracle. The real miracle was not that they had escaped the night; the real miracle was that someone would possibly agree to enter the night of their own accord because of the *mistake* of the other. That Bridget agreeing to meet Sly and love him at his own level.

I'll never forget when they told me that on that snowy Christmas Eve. It was the best Christmas gift I had ever received, the knowledge that they had broken their chains in the hot fires of their love. When they told me how, I knew what I had to do. They had found a cure for the most incurable, ignored disease in the world. I said that I had to do everything in my power to share the word.

What you are reading is the fruits of my labor. I have talked with them endlessly, written furiously, and done a phenomenal amount of thinking to produce this, and I write this as a message to all of you, whether constrained to the night or simply ignored in the daylight. Don't give up, don't ever give up. In seeking love on its own, you will lose yourself. But if you seek yourself, you shall find true love there waiting for you.

I sold Mike's after over a decade of owning the bar there, and took the money that was the fruit of years of patient labor. Then I set out into the night to spread the message of love that they had taught me:

That love had conquered despair, love had conquered mistakes, love had conquered the night. Love is real, and it calls to you.

In love,
JP Ligouri